'I'm so sorry

'No problem. We'

this morning.'

Amanda glanced up into a pair of smoky-blue eyes that made her heart miss a beat; smoky-blue eyes that shone out of the kind of sun-weathered face that a man gets when he spends as much of his time as possible out of doors.

Then he smiled. It was a lopsided, conspiratorial affair, a lift at one corner of his mouth that pulled the deep lines etched down his cheek into sharp relief.

'Why are you all over the place?' Amanda asked.

'We're a man short.' Daniel grinned. 'The driver booked for this job had to rush off to the hospital—his wife is having a baby.'

Baby. The word triggered that gooey feeling that had been with her for weeks. 'Her first?'

'Her fourth.'

Four babies. Amanda immediately found herself assailed by the image of four little bundles wrapped in white with blue ribbons, each one with smoky-blue eyes and a lopsided smile.

Born and raised in Berkshire, **Liz Fielding** started writing at the age of twelve when she won a hymn-writing competition at her convent school. After a gap of more years than she is prepared to admit to, during which she worked as a secretary in Africa and the Middle East, got married and had two children, she was finally able to realise her ambition and turn to full-time writing in 1992.

She now lives with her husband, John, in West Wales, surrounded by mystical countryside and romantic, crumbling castles, content to leave the travelling to her grown-up children and keeping in touch with the rest of the world via the Internet.

Recent titles by the same author:

A SUITABLE GROOM
DATING HER BOSS
AND MOTHER MAKES THREE

THE BABY PLAN

BY

LIZ FIELDING

MILLS & BOON

First published in Great Britain 1999
Harlequin Mills & Boon Limited,
Eton House, 18-24 Paradise Road, Richmond, Surrey TW9 1SR

ISBN 0 263 81908 6

Set in Times Roman 10½ on 12 pt.
02-0001-48609 C1

Printed and bound in Spain
by Litografia Rosés, S.A., Barcelona

CHAPTER ONE

'A BABY? You've decided to have a baby?' Amanda Garland Fleming said nothing, merely waited for her Business Manager to retrieve her chin from the office floor. '*Excuse me?*' Beth's laugh was definitely of the 'hold on—you're kidding me' variety. 'Have I missed something here? Something basic. Like a husband? Or a live-in partner? I didn't even know you were seeing someone. Not that seriously, anyway.' She glanced at the calendar. 'It's not April Fool's day, is it?'

Straight to the point. No messing. That was Beth.

Since the early autumn sunshine slanting through the window suggested that the question was purely rhetorical, Amanda ignored it. 'Could you ask Jane to pop out and pick up these books for me, when she has a moment?'

Beth's eyebrows rose sharply as she skimmed the list that contained every childcare book from Dr Spock to Penelope Leach. 'A little light…er…bed-time reading?'

'Research. I like to have a thorough grasp of the subject.'

'Then let's hope a "thorough grasp of the subject" is sufficient to bring you to your senses. You might even notice the flaw in your plan. Making a baby takes two, darling; not even the legendary organisational talent of Amanda Garland can manage that particular miracle single-handed.'

'On the contrary. The wonders of science ensure that a man—at least, the kind of man that requires nurturing, feeding and an endless supply of clean shirts—is now redundant.'

Beth's eyes sparked with mischief. 'Fun, though.'

Amanda knew better than to be drawn along that path. 'The books,' she repeated. 'And some folic acid.'

'Folic acid?'

'Vital for the healthy development of the neural tube. My *doctor* advised starting to take it before I get pregnant.'

'You've talked to your doctor about this? What did she say?'

'She said, ''Start taking folic acid.'''

Beth waited a moment, clearly hoping that she was going to laugh, say, *just kidding.* When it didn't happen she said, 'This isn't a joke is it? You're going to have a baby?'

Amanda had been in total control of her life since she was eighteen years old and had never once doubted a decision taken or looked back with regret. Now, a successful businesswoman on the cusp of her thirtieth year, she had taken stock of her life, considered where she wanted to be when the big four zero beckoned. She had already decided on changes to her business, on expansion into new areas, taking the Garland name out of the office and into the home. But that hadn't been enough.

'Well, it's still in the planning stage—'

'Planning stage!'

It was Amanda's turn to smile. 'You've heard of family planning, haven't you?' It was all going to be very simple. She wanted a child of her own, and with her thirtieth birthday looming on the horizon and her biological clock ticking with increasing urgency it was time to do what she was particularly good at. Make a plan, carry it through and achieve her goal. She had never needed a man to hold her hand before, and the advancement of science ensured that she could manage without one now.

Beth's expression, however, suggested that she didn't see it that way. 'You're talking about having a baby as if it's just another business deal. Have you any idea what motherhood will do to your life?'

'Well, yes. That's why I'm planning ahead. I've been giving a lot of thought to the problem of getting the right nanny.'

'*Nanny?*' Beth's voice rose a notch.

'Have you any idea how big the demand is? My sister-in-law's baby isn't due until the end of January, but Jilly has already started interviewing. It seems to me that it's an area crying out for the Garland touch.'

Beth grabbed the change of subject with both hands and ran with it. 'We have more work than we can handle just keeping up with the demand for our secretaries.' She paused. Amanda said nothing. 'Domestics, maybe,' she conceded, doubtfully. 'We'd need more staff, bigger offices, of course—'

'The ground-floor offices are becoming vacant shortly. They will be perfect.'

Beth opened her mouth, closed it again, then said, 'It's a specialised market, Amanda.'

The intercom buzzed from Reception. 'The driver wants to know how much longer he's going to have to wait, Miss Garland. The traffic warden is getting restive.'

'I'm coming now,' she said, rising to her feet, gathering her document case and her laptop.

'Amanda! You can't just leave...'

'We'll talk on Monday. I only mentioned it now because I want you to do a couple of things for me. Walk me down to the street.' She headed for the door. 'First, I want you to contact the Department of Employment and find out what, if any, regulations there are relating to the employment of nannies. And find out what you can about training, qualifications, that sort of thing.'

'And the second thing?'

Amanda pulled open the heavy glass street door. 'Give my doctor's office a call and ask her receptionist to make an appointment with the clinic for me.'

Daniel Redford, leaning against the bulk of the Mercedes, checked his watch impatiently and glanced up at the first-floor offices of the Garland Secretarial Agency. So much for the fabulous Garland Girls. They were reputed to be the classiest, best-qualified temps in town, but punctuality clearly wasn't one of their virtues.

'You going to be there much longer?' The traffic warden had already passed him once. Before he could answer, the door to the agency opened and his passenger emerged, all apologies.

'I'm *so* sorry to keep you waiting.' Daniel had a swift impression of gloss. Sleek, dark hair, a gleaming mouth, a pair of silvery grey eyes that included the traffic warden in a sunburst smile that would have won his dilatory passenger forgiveness for anything. 'I had a few loose ends to tie up.' Low and husky, her voice stroked against his skin like fur, and as she looked up at him Dan felt as if the ground was shifting dangerously beneath his feet.

She could tie him up any time. Hell, he'd have himself gift-wrapped and delivered…

Then, as Dan moved swiftly to open the car door, still reeling from the stunning effect of so much classy womanhood, he took the knock-out blow of her legs as she stepped up into the rear of the car. Legs clad in sheer black nylon beneath a skirt that did little more than peep from beneath the long line of her dark grey jacket—legs stretched almost to infinity by a pair of very high, very slender heels. The traffic warden saw them too, flashed him a grin that said 'lucky devil' before he shrugged and moved on.

Dan cleared his throat. 'No problem. We're all over the place ourselves this morning.'

'Are you?' Amanda, still enjoying the shocked look on Beth's face as she'd let the door swing shut, leaned across to put her laptop and document case on the seat. Then she realised that the driver still had the door open. She glanced up into a pair of smoky-blue eyes that for just a moment made her heart miss a beat; smoky-blue eyes that shone out of the kind of sun-weathered face that a man gets when he spends as much of his time as possible out of doors.

And that was before he smiled. It wasn't exactly a textbook smile. It was a lop-sided, conspiratorial affair, a lift at one corner of his mouth that pulled the deep lines etched down his cheeks into sharp relief. For some reason it made her think of a pirate with a cutlass between his teeth.

'Yes?' Her mouth felt as if she'd been chewing blotting paper.

'You won't forget your seat belt?' he prompted, before closing the door.

'What?' Then, 'Oh, yes.' A deeply caring pirate. She gave herself a firm, mental shake and clicked the seat belt into place. 'Why?' she asked as he eased himself into the driving seat and started the powerful engine before glancing over his shoulder at the traffic.

'Why what?'

'Why are you all over the place?' She found such details interesting. It was paying attention to those kind of details that had made her so successful. And she wanted to keep him talking.

'We're a man short,' he explained, as he waited for a gap in the traffic. 'The driver booked for this job had to rush off to the hospital.'

'An accident?'

'I wouldn't care to comment on that.' He grinned. 'His wife is having a baby.'

Baby. The word triggered that gooey feeling that had been with her for weeks. She'd put on that high-powered, organised career woman faćade this morning because it was the only way she knew how to handle it. Beth was the gooey one. The one who fell in love at the drop of a hat, who sighed over babies. She'd thought she was immune.

Then her brother had announced that his new wife was pregnant.

Her mother had been so thrilled at the prospect of finally becoming a grandmother after giving up hope of either of her children doing the decent thing. *She'd* been delighted, too. After brushing aside that infinitesimal moment of chilling emptiness, of something that might just have been envy.

Brushed it aside, but not away. It had refused to

leave her, which was probably why she had found herself in the baby department of a nearby department store a few days later, looking for a suitable gift for her first niece or nephew. Something pretty to decorate the nursery being prepared for the new baby.

She had only intended to spend ten minutes picking out some fluffy toy. Then she'd seen this tiny pair of velvet baby boots. White. Soft as down. With the littlest turn-back cuff.

A baby. 'Her first?' Amanda asked, on an odd little catch of breath, in a voice she scarcely recognised as her own.

'Her fourth.'

Four babies. Amanda immediately found herself assailed by the image of four little bundles wrapped in white with blue ribbons, each one with smoky-blue eyes and a lop-sided smile. That was how it had been for weeks. Just the word was enough to trigger all kinds of fantasies.

'She's done it three times and she still needs her husband to hold her hand? How pathetic,' she said, her tongue firmly in her cheek. *How romantic,* the unexpectedly soft centre whispered.

Daniel turned his head a little further and saw that his lovely passenger was smiling. Encouraged, he said, 'To be honest, I think it's more a case of her holding his.' An hour ago Dan had been cursing the woman for going into labour early when they were so busy, forcing him to cancel a meeting and take out one of the cars himself. Quite suddenly he was prepared to take the philosophical view. 'Men are such wimps.'

'I'll take your word for it.' Not that she believed he was a wimp. Not for a minute. Not even the crisply efficient Miss Garland thought that. And her soft centre was absolutely certain that he would be a tower of strength, holding her hand, wiping her brow, reminding her when to breathe, when to pant. *Stop it, right now!* she ordered her hyperactive imagination. Then, as he waited for an opening in the seemingly endless string of traffic, she made a determined effort to pull herself together, concentrate on the matter in hand. 'How long will it take to get to The Beeches? Can we make it by ten?'

'I'll do my best, but I'm running short of miracles for this week.'

Her groan was heartfelt. She should have left the minute the car had arrived, but she'd needed to sound out Beth. Without her support the whole thing would be a lot more complicated. She was going to need *someone* to mop her brow and hold her hand. Modern science might offer the perfect solution to her needs, but it wouldn't be there to offer any of those extras, any of those tender touches.

'Relax. If Miss Garland gives you a hard time for being late just suggest she tries driving through Knightsbridge at this time in the morning.' His eyes crinkled in another of those killer smiles.

Miss Garland? He didn't know? Didn't realise who she was? It was her turn to smile.

'And who shall I say sent the message?'

There was a hint of laughter in her voice and Dan glanced again at the mirror to check out what that mouth was doing. Actually, her mouth was worth looking at just for itself. Scarlet red and sexy as hell. 'Daniel Redford. At your service, ma'am.'

'I'll be sure to tell her, Daniel Redford. In the

meantime, since you're at my service, will you please do your best to get me there on time?'

'I'll certainly try,' he said, and, glancing over his shoulder, edged the car away from the kerb, forcing a cab driver to give way to him. The cab driver did not like it and expressed his feelings forcefully. Dan merely smiled and raised a hand in a gesture of thanks, as if the cabbie had given way politely. 'I've heard she's a bit of an old tartar,' he said. 'Your Miss Garland.'

'Have you?' The lady with the beautiful mouth seemed surprised. 'Who told you that?'

'She's famous for it. Efficiency with a capital E. Are you a new girl?'

'Er… no.' The tartar in question wondered briefly what he would say if she told him the truth. She resisted the temptation. This was far more entertaining. 'I've been with the agency since the very beginning.'

'Oh, well, you'll know all about her. What's she like?'

'I thought you knew all about her.'

He shrugged. 'Only gossip.'

'And the gossips say that she's a tartar? No, wait, an *efficient* tartar.'

'A very rich, efficient tartar I would imagine, if she charges the kind of fees that include chauffeur driven cars for her secretaries.'

He was making it up as he went along, she decided. Just to keep her talking. The thought made her want to smile. She tried very hard not to. 'Her standards are certainly very high.'

'I don't suppose she'd approve of one her "girls" chatting with a common chauffeur, then?'

As long as they looked the part and did a good job,

her 'girls' could chatter to whomsoever they wished, in their own time. '*Are* you common?' she asked.

Amanda didn't think so for a minute. His accent was pure London, but the streets had been pretty effectively scrubbed from it. And from the brief impression she'd had of him as he'd opened the door, waited for her to fasten her seat belt, she knew that few men of her acquaintance could have matched him for physical presence. He topped her by a head, with shoulders that could have borne the troubles of the world and the kind of bone structure that gave a face character. She catalogued his attributes and found none of them wanting. And there had been something distinctly uncommon about those eyes.

It occurred to Amanda that if she had been looking for a man, rather than a sperm donation, she would be hard pressed to find a more attractive proposition. The thought settled low in her abdomen and lingered there.

Was he common? It wasn't the answer Daniel had expected, but it was certainly the one he deserved. He'd made the kind of remark that would leave a girl appearing snobbish, feeling uncomfortable if she didn't answer, chose not to engage in conversation. Hardly the way to treat a paying customer, even if someone else was doing the paying.

He was pleased that she hadn't fallen for it, but then his passenger was hardly a girl. She was a self-assured and very beautiful woman, far too mature to be taken in by that kind of line—by any kind of line for that matter. Looking the way she did, she was bound to have heard them all before. It would take originality to catch this lady's attention, to hold it. It occurred to him that it was a long time since he'd met a woman capable of holding his.

'I was a docklands brat,' he said, leaving it for her to decide. 'In the days when there were still docks worthy of the name.' He still was, he realised, and smiled at the thought. He hadn't moved very far from his roots.

'In the days before the warehouses were bought by developers and converted into luxury homes for the seriously rich?' He had been direct, assuming that the truth would put a brake on the conversation, but her mouth widened in another of those smiles. 'A bit of a tearaway, were you?'

Got it in one. 'I'm a model citizen these days,' he assured her.

'Mmm.'

The sound portrayed a world of doubt and Daniel laughed. Flirting was a bit like riding a bicycle; there might be a bit of a wobble when you hadn't done it for a while, but it soon came back.

'What about you?' he asked.

Nice teeth, Amanda thought, looking at his smile reflected in the rear view mirror. Then gave herself a mental slap for checking him out feature by feature. As if she were looking over a stud horse. *Nice mouth.* 'Am I a model citizen?'

'That's a given; after all you're a Garland Girl. Highly trained, beautifully groomed and guaranteed trustworthy.'

Her shoulders lifted half a centimetre. The public relations image was still in place and doing the job, she was happy to note. It was the quality image she intended to exploit to the full with her plans for expansion. 'I told you, Miss Garland has very high standards.'

'Bad-tempered old tartars always use that excuse.' Stuck fast in rush hour traffic, with nothing to do but look in his mirror at his passenger, he saw her mouth begin to form a protest, then give a little half-smile as if she were secretly amused by his less than flattering description of her boss, but she refused to join in. 'How did you get to be one of the famous Garlands Girls?' he prompted.

She'd been born to it, that was how. Garland had been her mother's maiden name and she'd suggested that Amanda use it when she started the agency, rather than the family name of Fleming, just in case it had all gone pear-shaped. She'd been irritated at the time by this apparent lack of faith, but then a journalist doing a feature on secretarial agencies had coined the phrase 'Garland Girls' to describe her particular brand of educated, classy temps and it had stuck—become a brand-name almost. She was seriously thinking of trademarking it.

But she wasn't about to tell this flirtatious chauffeur any of that. No matter how attractive his mouth, or uncommon his eyes. Or wicked his smile. 'I took a secretarial course so that I could help my father. When he didn't need me any more, I looked around for something else to do.' Well, it was the truth, as far as it went.

'I suppose if you're going to be a temp, you might as well work for the best,' he agreed.

'Even if the boss is a bad-tempered old tartar?' She saw his eyes reflected in the rearview mirror. He was looking straight at her and for just a moment she thought he knew, that he had simply been teasing her.

Then the traffic began to move and he looked away as he eased the car forward.

'Don't you have any ambitions beyond temping?'

More than ambitions. Plans. Business plans and personal plans. And today she had put them into action. 'Is all you ever wanted to be a driver?' she countered.

Well, he'd asked for that, Daniel reflected. And when you came right down to it they both worked for other people by the hour. 'I get to meet some interesting people that way,' he said. And meant it.

'So do I.'

There was something about that voice, something soft and warm that curled around his gut and settled there like a warm puppy. He looked again in the mirror, couldn't stop himself, but all he could see was her mouth, full and shining and very kissable.

Kissable? This was getting out of hand. He readjusted the mirror, slipped on a pair of dark glasses and decided it would be a whole lot more sensible to keep his entire attention fixed on the rear of the car in front. His mouth couldn't have been wired up to the sensible part of his brain, though. 'Sometimes I even get to know their names,' he said, encouragingly.

'Do you?' Amanda had wondered how long it would be before he got around to asking her name and she had looked forward to telling him. Looked forward to saying, *I'm Amanda Garland. The old tartar. How d'you do?* Watch him flinch. Instead she found herself saying, 'I'm Mandy Fleming.'

Well, so she was. Her father had called her Mandy. Her brother still did. And Garland, after all, was just her professional name. Her company name. The old tartar's name.

'Isn't that the old tartar's name?'

His words echoed the ones in her head, mocking her. He had known all along… Who was going to look the idiot now?

'Isn't that your boss's name?' he repeated, when she didn't reply. 'Amanda Garland? Mandy's short for Amanda isn't it?'

Amanda released the breath she had been holding a touch too long. Why else would she feel breathless? 'No one ever calls her anything but Miss Garland when I'm around,' she said, with feeling. Except Beth, but they had been together since the beginning. She'd been the first temp she taken on her books and within a week had been running the office for her.

'Definitely not a Mandy, eh?'

He had put on a pair of dark glasses and his eyes were hidden. 'Not in the office,' she agreed.

He stopped talking then, as the traffic began to move, and gave the business of getting out of London his full attention. For a moment she watched his hands as he manoeuvred the big car through the busy morning streets, then with a start she dragged her attention away, opened her laptop, switched it on, began to make some notes. But she found concentration tougher than usual. It had been so long since her heart-rate had picked up for anything except a workout at the gym that she'd almost forgotten how it felt.

She glanced out of the window at the relentless tedium of grey concrete office buildings as they sped along the Chiswick flyover. Nothing to distract her there, so she gave up trying to avoid staring at the back of Daniel Redford's neck. He didn't wear a cap, or uniform of any kind. The car hire company he worked for apparently dressed their drivers in well-cut grey double-breasted suits, a white shirt and burgundy tie with the company logo. Smart but unobtrusive. She made a note to think about what Garland nannies might wear.

Daniel's bulk filled his suit to perfection. His light brown hair was skilfully cut, not too short, layered into his neck and brightened by the sun. Nice profile, too, what she could see of it from this angle. He had a good jaw line, hard cheekbones, and she remembered the kind of nose that looked as if it had lived life head-on. Not particularly pretty, but strong, like his big hands, with their long, square-tipped fingers, neatly trimmed nails. They held the wheel lightly, but he was a man in complete control of his environment, a man who would be in complete control of anything he touched…

'Have you worked for Capitol Cars for long?' she asked, distracting herself from the disturbing direction in which her thoughts were heading.

'Twenty years.'

'Really?' His cheeks had moved so that she knew he was smiling, and even though he'd adjusted his mirror so that she could no longer see his mouth she remembered the lazy lift to one corner, the deep crease that had appeared like magic down his cheek as he had swept open the door for her. He was a heartbreaker and no mistake. And undoubtedly married; his kind always were. Forget it, Amanda, she told herself firmly. Stick to the plan. 'You must enjoy the work, then.'

'I suppose I must.' She saw him glance at the mirror. Was he looking at her, or the traffic behind them?

With his eyes hidden behind dark glasses it was impossible to tell. 'The tips are good, too. I was given a couple of theatre tickets the other day.' He mentioned the new musical that had opened to rave reviews a few weeks earlier.

'That's quite some tip. I've heard the tickets are like gold dust.' Then she realised that he might think she was angling for an invitation. Maybe she was… 'What was it like?' she asked, quickly.

'I've no idea.'

'You don't like the theatre?' Or maybe his wife didn't like the theatre. Not that he was wearing a ring. But then, these days it didn't have to be marriage. A good-looking man in his late thirties, early forties was scarcely likely to be living alone. Not if he was straight. *Oh, please let him be straight!*

'They're for next week. What about you?'

'What? Oh, the theatre.' She swallowed. 'Love it,' she said, her heart leaping into overdrive as she anticipated his next question. He didn't ask it. Definitely spoken for, she told herself as he mentioned a couple of plays he'd seen. Not that it mattered. Right now she needed to keep her life as simple as possible. Complications in the form of a sexy chauffeur were not in the plan. 'I saw that,' she interrupted. 'It was incredible. Did you see…?'

Their tastes seemed to have a pleasant syncronicity. He might have been a dockland brat but he obviously appreciated good theatre. 'I went to Pavarotti-in-the-Park, a couple of years ago,' he said, after a while. 'It rained all through, but it was worth it. Do you like that sort of stuff?'

Amanda had avoided mentioning opera, which would teach her to be such a damned snob, she thought. 'Yes. I was there under my umbrella.' Then, in for a penny, she thought. 'I like the ballet, too.'

He wrinkled up his battered nose. 'No. Sorry. There's passion in opera. Ballet…' He left her to fill in the blank.

'Maybe you just haven't seen the right ballet,' she persisted.

'Maybe.' He sounded doubtful. 'I like football, though.'

'I think I'll stick to ballet, thanks all the same.'

She saw his jaw lift in a smile. 'Maybe you should try it before you judge.'

Touché. 'What about your wife?'

Damn! She hadn't meant to say that. Now he would know she was fishing.

'My wife?' He paused as they approached roadworks, concentrated on dealing with a busy contraflow of traffic.

'Does she like football?' Amanda held her breath. Her heart stopped beating.

'I've never met a woman who does,' he said. *So? What did that mean? As if she didn't know.* 'We're almost there,' he said, as they threaded through the cones and down the sliproad. 'It looks like you'll be on time after all.'

'Wonderful.' Fine. Perfect. Her head continued to churn out adjectives, none of which were wonderful, or fine, or perfect. In fact every one of them would have had Beth's eyebrows glued to the ceiling.

For some minutes they sped through thickly wooded lanes, conversation at an end. Amanda, finding it essential to do something with her hands, reknotted the silk scarf at her throat, closed her laptop, gathered her case. By the time Daniel stopped in front of the portico of one of the most expensive hotels in England, she was ready to step out of the car and walk away. It was only determination to prove to herself that she was not desperate to escape that kept her in her seat, waiting for him to open the door for her.

Daniel slipped off the dark glasses, tucked them into his breast pocket, then walked around to open the door. High heels and gravel were a treacherous mix, and he offered his hand as she swung her legs out of the car. She placed her cool fingers on his without hesitation and straightened with all the poise of a model. All part of the 'Garland Girls' training, no doubt. 'We've made it with two minutes to spare. You won't get your wrist slapped by the dragon lady, after all,' he said.

Only a man could be that patronising, Amanda decided, then amended the thought to a *married* man. A married man whose strong, work-hardened fingers were curled protectively about her own.

She very carefully removed her hand from his and glanced at her wristwatch to check the time. 'Thank you, Daniel,' she said, formally.

'My pleasure, Miss Fleming.' He moved to close the car door. 'I'll see you this evening.'

'Will you?' Her breath stilled in expectation.

'At five.'

Of course. Why else would he see her? He had a wife. It was just as well. It wasn't as if she needed him. Not for hard-to-get theatre tickets, not for anything. She could get her own tickets for any show in town, and all she had to do was click her fingers and half a dozen men would be fighting to lend her an arm, and anything else she wanted, for the evening.

Unfortunately she had never been able to work up

much enthusiasm for any man who could be brought to heel like an eager puppy with his tongue hanging out, which was why she was making her own arrangements for the 'anything else'.

But right now she was the one with her tongue dragging on the floor and it was definitely time to haul it back in.

'I'll try not to keep you waiting again,' she said briskly, and walked into the hotel without a backward glance.

Daniel watched Mandy Fleming walk away from him. It wasn't exactly a hardship. Those long legs moved her body along in the way a woman should be moved, slow and sexy. A woman's walk said a lot about her. Mandy Fleming's said confidence, style. But that straight back told him something else. She was feeling decidedly put out that he hadn't asked her to go to the theatre with him. She'd have said no, but she'd expected to be asked. And he smiled to himself. How did that old saying go? Make 'em laugh, make 'em cry, make 'em wait? He didn't have much time for men who made women cry, but the other two… His smile broadened as he drove towards the gates of the hotel. Like riding a bicycle.

The morning dragged, endlessly. The afternoon was, if anything, worse, and Amanda had a hard time keeping herself focused as she gave her own presentation on the benefits of employing temporary staff. Just the slightest lapse in concentration and her mind was wandering off to dwell on smoky blue eyes and broad shoulders, good hands and a sexy smile, all carried on two well-muscled legs.

Two well-muscled, *married* legs.

CHAPTER TWO

DANIEL headed for the airport, picked up his passenger, delivered him to his hotel in Piccadilly and drove back to the garage. The traffic was a nightmare but he was working on automatic, his head full of Mandy Fleming.

How long had it been since a woman had stayed in his head for more than five minutes? How long had it been since he couldn't wait to renew the acquaintance? But then Miss Fleming was one stylish lady. Those legs. That mouth.

His brows drew together as his thoughts strayed to the way she dressed. She had expensive tastes for a secretary. Even a top-of-the-range, seriously expensive Garland Agency secretary who merited a chauffeur-driven car.

Yet there had been something in her voice, something in her smile that had made his skin prickle with excitment. And the air had positively crackled with electricity when she'd put her hand on his for that briefest of touches. Oh, she'd been cool, her back ramrod-straight, but he knew she'd felt it too. The care with which she had removed her fingers from his had been too studied for anything else.

Then he pulled a face. Mandy Fleming wasn't the kind of woman to be interested in a chauffeur. Well-educated, lovely to look at, she was the kind of secretary who would have her eyes firmly fixed on the boss rather than one of the bit-players. The thought brought an ironic smile to his lips, a smile that quickly faded.

Things had been so straightforward when he had been struggling to make a living with a one-car business. If a girl had smiled at him then he'd been sure that it wasn't his money she was smiling at. All that had changed the day he'd bought a second car and taken on his first employee.

He pulled into the valeting area. 'Any news from the hospital, Bob?'

'It's a girl, boss. Mother and baby doing well.' There was nothing wrong with the words, just something about the way Bob said them that alerted him to trouble.

'So what's the problem?' he asked.

Bob didn't lift his gaze from the coach-built bodywork he was stroking to an eye-dazzling shine; he simply jerked his grey head in the direction of the office. 'Sadie arrived about half an hour ago. She's in the office.'

Dan said something short and scatological.

'It's not half-term is it?'

'No.'

The older man straightened, wadded his duster, squinted along the gleaming bonnet. 'Thought not.'

No one was eager to meet his eye as he strode through the yard and into the office. As he set eyes on his daughter, he could see why.

She was sitting in his chair with her knee-high Doc Martens propped defiantly upon his desk. Her clothes, black to a stitch, could only have come from some charity shop, and her hair, shoulder-length and gleaming chestnut the last time he had seen her, had been cropped and dyed the kind of black from which no light escaped. Her face, in contrast, was dead white, her eyes rimmed with heavy black lines, her nails painted to match. She looked as if she was auditioning for the role of Morticia Addams but had forgotten the glamour, and it was all he could do to prevent himself from flinching. Since that was undoubtedly the effect she was striving to achieve, he made the effort.

He'd hoped that this was simply a day-trip, an excursion, a little French leave from the boarding school that charged a queen's ransom to turn the daughters of those who could afford the fees into the very best they could be, academically and socially—and, in his daughter's case, were fighting a losing battle. One look was all it had taken to quell any such notion.

'Mercedes,' he murmured, acknowledging her presence as he helped himself to coffee from the machine his secretary kept permanently on the go. Sadie hated being called that. She knew as well as he did that her name had been Vickie's idea of a joke, a constant reminder that he'd had to cancel the Mercedes he'd had on order when he'd discovered that he was about to become a father. But right now he wasn't in the mood to indulge his daughter with pet names. 'I didn't realise you had a holiday.' He lifted her boot-clad feet from his desk and dropped them to the floor before turning his diary round to check the entries against the date. 'No, you're not here. It's not like Karen to make a mistake—'

'I didn't think I had to make an appointment to see my own father.' Sadie pushed the chair back and stood up. Dear God, she seemed to grow six inches each time he saw her. Guilt suggested that was because he didn't see her often enough. But that was her choice. Apart from a grudging week at the cottage, she'd spent the entire summer with school-friends.

'You don't. Just lately it's been the other way around.'

'Yes, well, that's all about to change. I've been suspended from school,' she declared defiantly. 'And you might as well know, I've no intention of going back.' He made no comment. 'You can't make me.'

He was well aware of that fact. She was sixteen, and if she refused to go back to school there was precious little he could do about it except point out the pitfalls of cutting short her education.

'You've re-sits in November,' he reminded her calmly. The expletive that told him what he could with his re-sits would have earned him boxed ears from his mother at that age. But then Sadie didn't have a mother, at least not one who cared to be reminded that she had a daughter rapidly approaching womanhood, so he ignored the bad language, as he had ignored her appearance. She was doing her level best to shock him, make him angry. He was both, but he knew better than to show it. 'You won't be able to do anything without English and maths.'

'You didn't bother about exams—'

'Nobody cared what I did, Sadie. Does Mrs Warburton know where you are?' He mentioned her headmistress before she could point out that her mother didn't care much about her own firstborn, either.

'No. I was sent to my room to wait until someone could spare the time to bring me home. They probably think I'm still there.' She threw back her head and laughed. 'They'll be running around like headless chickens when they realise I've gone.'

He pressed the intercom. 'Karen, call Mrs Warburton at Dower House and let her know that Sadie is with me.'

'Yes, Dan.'

'Then will you organise some flowers and fruit for Brian's wife—'

'I've already taken care of it. And Ned Gresham's agreed to come in and cover for him.' Karen might not have the glamour of a Garland Girl, but she was their equal in every other way. Dan recalled Mandy's smile, slightly parted lips, the way her fingers had felt as they had rested briefly on his and the way his skin had tightened at the contact. Not quite every way, which was probably just as well. A sexy secretary combined with a garage full of impressionable drivers and mechanics was nothing short of a recipe for disaster. 'Do you want me to write him in for the five o'clock pick-up from The Beeches?' She didn't say, *Now that Sadie's arrived.* She didn't need to.

With just a touch of regret, he surrendered the memory, the anticipated pleasure… But not to Ned Gresham. With his public school accent and chiselled good looks, the man thought he was God's gift to women. A lot of women thought that too. The idea of him flirting with Mandy Fleming… 'No. Ask Bob to do it.' He kept his finger on the button for a moment. 'Tell him he can take Miss Fleming home rather than back to the Garland offices if she prefers.'

Karen laughed. 'Pretty, was she?'

'Simple public relations, Karen. Please the secretary and you've got the boss.'

'And if Miss Fleming lives on the other side of London?'

'She'll be even more impressed and Bob will enjoy the overtime.'

'She was *that* pretty?'

'I didn't notice.' His lie was rewarded with the disbelieving snort it merited before he flicked the switch. Dan straightened and looked at his daughter, remembering the pretty child she had been, seeing the lovely woman she would become once she stopped trying to hurt him, hurt herself—but only because her mother wasn't around to take the abuse in person. 'Come on,' he said.

'I'm not going back,' she repeated stubbornly.

'I heard you, Sadie. I'm not taking you back to school, but I'm not leaving you to run around London on your own. If you're not going back to school you're going to have to work for a living.'

'Work?' Sadie's careless certainty, the belief that she was the one calling the shots, wavered. That gave Dan hope.

'You leave school; you have three choices. If you've decided not to do re-sits, college is a non-starter. The alternative is work, and since you're hardly likely to have employers lining up for the privilege of signing you up, you'll have to work for me.' He waited for her reaction. When none was forthcoming he added, 'Of course you're welcome to try the Job Centre if you think you can do better?'

'You said three choices.'

'You could telephone your mother and see if she'll offer you a home.' He had his fingers mentally crossed. The last thing he wanted for Sadie was a lotus-eating existence with her mother. 'I don't suppose she would expect you to work for your living.'

Her response left no room for doubt about Sadie's feelings on the subject. Daniel hadn't anticipated ever feeling sorry for his ex-wife, yet for a woman to have earned so much scorn from her own daughter would wring sympathy from a stone. 'No? Well, it's not too late to change your mind.' His gaze rested momentarily on her hair. 'Assuming the suspension is not as permanent as your hair colour.'

'Read my lips, Dad.' She pointed a black-painted fingernail at her mouth and said, very slowly and very carefully, 'I am not going back to school.'

'Are you going to tell me why? Or are you going to wait for Mrs Warburton's letter to arrive? I imagine she will write to me.'

'Yeah.' Her voice was all careless indifference, but her gaze slid away from him as she stuffed a hand into the pocket of her black leather bomber jacket and tossed a crumpled envlope onto the desk. Not so tough as she would have him believe, his little girl, and his insides turned over; it was all he could do to stop himself from grabbing her and hugging her and telling her that it didn't matter, that whatever she'd done it didn't matter because he loved her.

By the time she had gathered herself sufficiently to fix him with a belligerent glare, he was looking out of the window, contemplating the yard as if he had nothing more on his mind than the price of engine oil. He ignored the letter. 'I'd rather hear it from you.' His tone was mild, but his heart was beating like a steam pump. 'Was it drink?' he prompted. 'Boys?' He turned to look at her, his mouth suddenly bone-dry. 'Drugs?'

'What do you take me for?'

An average teenage girl with more money than was good for her and a desperate need to lash out, to hurt the people who loved her.

'I've been suspended for a week, that's all.' Under

the white make-up he could have sworn she blushed. 'For dying my hair, if you must know.'

It had to be relief that made him want to laugh. 'Just for dying your hair? Mrs Warburton isn't usually that harsh.' Surely living with the colour while it grew out would be punishment enough. 'Is she?' he demanded sharply, suddenly very sure that she wasn't telling the whole truth.

Sadie lifted her shoulders in a couldn't-care-less shrug. 'Yes, well, when the Warthog had me in her office to haul me over the coals for ''letting down the high standards of Dower House School'' …' she affected a nasal twang that was a cruel caricature of Mrs Warburton's aristocratic accent '… I suggested it was time she touched up her own roots because the grey was showing.'

He put down his cup, turned away, his lips curled hard against his teeth. 'I can see how that might not have helped matters,' he said, when he was sure he wouldn't betray himself.

'Hypocritical old cow.'

He was forced to cover his mouth, pretend to cough. 'Maybe so, but that really wasn't very kind.'

'She shouldn't have made such a big deal about it. Anyone would think I'd had my nose pierced, or something.'

'That's banned too, is it?'

'Everything's banned. Of course if I'm not going back, I suppose I could—'

'Your mother had her nose pierced the last time I saw her,' he said. 'She was wearing a diamond stud.'

Sadie said nothing; she didn't have to. Dan knew she wasn't about to do anything that would make her look more like her mother than she already did. Or had done, until she'd dyed her hair. That was something to be grateful for.

'So, when do I start this wonderful job, then?'

Her tone was as belligerent as her expression, but adolescent rebellion was something he knew all about; this wasn't the moment to demand she apologise. Despite the 'hard girl' act, he was sure she didn't need to be told what was required, whether she returned to school or not. He was also sure that she was more likely to get on with it if she wasn't nagged.

'No time like the present. Come on, I'll get you an overall and then we'll go and find Bob.'

'I can't wait.' The heavy sarcasm suggested that this was going to be a long week. He just hoped, for both their sakes, that at the end of it Sadie would realise that school was a soft option compared with working for a living. And that Mrs Warburton was in a forgiving mood.

Should he have tried harder to persuade her to go back? What would her mother have done? Not much. Vickie was in the Bahamas with her latest lover and a new baby to drool over. He doubted if she would welcome a phone call reminding her that she had a daughter approaching an age at which she would become competition. Instinct suggested that his best bet was to set Sadie to work and hope that a week of mind-numbing drudgery would do the job for him.

'What am I going to have to do?'

'The options are limited since you can't drive—'

'I can drive,' she declared fiercely. 'Better than most people.'

That was true. He'd taught her to drive in the field behind the cottage he had bought a couple of years back, and she could handle a motorbike or a car with all the panache of a professional. 'You can't drive a car on the road until you're seventeen, Sadie. You can't even move one across the yard until you have your licence because you wouldn't be insured.' She didn't answer, but it was obvious that calling her bluff was not going to have any immediate effect. 'Perhaps you should try a bit of everything. Make yourself useful about the place.'

'Be a dogsbody, you mean?' She was not impressed. 'Great.'

'If you plan on running this outfit one day you might as well find out how everything works.'

'Who said I was?' she demanded.

'If you don't go to college you won't have much choice. You can start in the garage with Bob. He'll show you the ropes.'

'Cleaning cars.' Only an adolescent could endow two such inoffensive words with quite that level of scorn. 'You didn't start this business by cleaning cars.'

'I started with one car, Sadie, and I promise you, it didn't clean itself.'

'Very funny.'

'You think you're such a catch? Come back when you've seen what the Job Centre has to offer and we'll talk again.'

'But you're my father; you can't expect me to skivvy for you…' Something in his expression must have warned her that she was doing herself no favours, because she stopped. 'Okay, okay, whatever you say.'

If only. 'And one other thing, Sadie. During working hours you're no different from anyone else around here, you're an employee with the same privileges and the same responsibilities. That means you arrive on time—'

'That won't be difficult. Just give me a call five minutes before you leave.'

'I don't provide a wake-up service for my staff, Sadie. And I don't give them a lift to work, either. The only place I'm prepared to drive you to is Dower House, next Monday morning.'

'Don't bother. I'm sure there's a bus.'

'There is.' He was looking out of the window, contemplating the business that he had built from scratch. It had been hard. Twenty-four hours a day work, and worry that had left him with too little time to invest in his marriage, too distracted by his own big ideas to notice when his wife had gone looking for company elsewhere. Or perhaps he'd needed the big ideas and the twenty-four-hour work schedule to distract him from his marriage. He turned to his errant daughter. 'And while you're here,' he instructed, 'you'll do anything Bob asks of you. In return you get as much tea and coffee as you can drink, a cooked lunch in the café next door and clean overalls every morning. I'm afraid you have to be eighteen before you can join the pension scheme.'

'My dad, the comedian.'

'Your *boss*, the comedian. At least while you're at the garage.'

'You're kidding, right?' He didn't bother to reply. 'Okay… *boss*. How much do I get paid for doing the dirty work around here?'

'The going rate for the job. After deductions for tax and national insurance you might earn almost as much as your allowance.'

'Do I still get the allowance?'

'What do you think?'

Amanda couldn't wait for five o'clock. She had been looking forward to attending this seminar, but it had proved mind-numbingly dull. Or maybe it was just that her mind had other things to occupy it. A pair of capable hands. A quiff of sun-bleached hair with a will of its own. A dangerously attractive smile that still made her feel warm inside. Ridiculous.

Well, she was being ridiculous all round today. Common sense suggested it would have been wiser to call Capitol and cancel that five o'clock car. Her mother lived only a few miles away; she could have got a taxi there, stayed the night. Stayed the weekend, even. Except that she wasn't quite ready to share her plans.

And now she'd left it too late.

She emerged from the hotel and glanced around, looking for Daniel, expecting to see him leaning against the bulk of his car. He wasn't. Maybe he'd expected her to be late again, because the big dark blue Mercedes was on the far side of the car park and he was sitting inside it. Oh, well. She pinned a bright, careless smile in place and crossed the gravel. In the event, it was unnecessary, because the man who looked up from the driver's seat was not Daniel Redford.

The plunging sense of disappointment certainly put that careless smile in its place. She definitely cared. Which was pretty stupid since she had only met the man once. Apparently that didn't matter as much as she'd thought it did.

'Yes, miss?' The man had made no move to get

out and open the car door for her, and for a moment she floundered before finding her voice.

'You are from Capitol Cars, aren't you? I didn't realise I'd have a different driver.'

'You haven't got a different driver.' She swung around at the sound of Daniel's voice. 'You have a different car, which is probably why you didn't see me.'

How could she have missed him? He must have seen her confusion because he was smiling as he took her arm. 'I'm parked over there.' Her eyes widened as she took in the opulent lines of a classic wine-red Jaguar parked on the far side of the hotel entrance. She'd been so intent on looking for a Mercedes, for Daniel, that she hadn't even noticed it. Amanda smiled apologetically at the driver of the Mercedes and walked with Daniel across to his car. 'Well, this *is* different,' she said.

'Someone rear-ended the Mercedes this afternoon.'

Concern brought her to a halt and she looked up at him anxiously. 'Were you hurt?'

'Hurt?' Then he shook his head. 'Oh, no. I wasn't driving it when it happened.' They reached the car. 'I hope you don't mind this old jalopy.'

'Mind?' She glanced at him. 'Why should I mind? She's absolutely beautiful. A real classic.' Whether the Jaguar merited quite that amount of breathy admiration was a moot point. But Amanda needed some excuse for her breathlessness.

'Well, I'm glad you like her because there is a bit of a problem.' Then he did that thing with the smile that made simple breathlessness seem like a piece of cake. 'Because she's rather mature, there are no seat belts in the rear, so you'll have to sit up front with me.'

'That's not a problem. That's a pleasure.' She surrendered her laptop and document case to Daniel, and as he opened the door for her she stepped into the leather-scented interior. 'My father had a car like this,' she said, when he joined her. 'It was dark green.'

'The height of luxury in its time.'

'It's still luxury. A real treat after a dull day.'

'I wish I'd had a dull day.' There was a world of feeling in his voice as he started the car.

'A baby and a rear-ending. Yes, I can see how that might complicate your life.'

'They were the easy problems. After all, the baby isn't mine and someone else's insurance company will be paying for the damage to the car.'

'There's more?'

'They say things happen in threes. My daughter chose today to drop out of school.'

His daughter. 'I'm sorry,' she said. And she meant it. In more ways than one. The happy haze evaporated as quickly as it had formed at the sound of his voice. He had a daughter. Well, what was the big surprise in that? She'd asked about his wife and he'd been evasive. She should have remembered that before she'd made an utter fool of herself with her stupid *That's a pleasure…*

Well, that would teach her to let her mind go a-wandering. He had a wife, and a wife almost inevitably meant children. But the inevitability of it didn't stop her heart from sinking like a soggy sponge.

'Was there any special reason?' she asked. Well, she had to say something. 'For the dropping out?'

'She flunked her GCSEs last summer. I'm hoping she's just a bit fed up because all her friends have moved on to the sixth form while she's stuck with re-sits.' Daniel pulled out of the parking bay and headed for the gates.

'Hoping?'

'I suspect it may be a symptom of something worse.' There was what seemed like an endless pause as he reached the gates, waited for the traffic, then pulled out into the lane.

She couldn't ask. Could she? 'A symptom?' Amanda prompted, once they were cruising.

Daniel Redford glanced at her briefly. Then, as if coming to a decision, he said, 'Her mother abandoned her when she was eight years old. The divorce was a long time ago, but I have the feeling that it's finally caught up with her.'

'Oh, I am sorry.' And she was. She might be glad that Daniel was unattached. The soggy sponge might be making a miraculous recovery. But she couldn't be happy that a little girl had been abandoned by her mother. 'That's a terrible thing to happen to any child. What'll you do?'

'With Sadie?' He glanced across at her and quite unexpectedly grinned. Sadie might have taken her mother's abandonment hard, but she didn't get the feeling that Daniel Redford was too bothered. 'I've put her to work cleaning cars at the garage. I'm hoping a week of that might help to change her mind.'

'It would certainly send me scurrying back to my books. But shouldn't you be at home with her now, helping her sort out her life, instead of chauffeuring me about the place?'

'I should. In fact you were rescheduled for another

driver, but what with the shunt and a baggage handlers' strike delaying a couple of airport jobs, it all got a bit complicated. Don't worry about it. I've no doubt she's very grateful for the opportunity to avoid me for another hour or two.'

Amanda was grateful too. So grateful that she sent a silent thank you to the striking airport baggage handlers, wherever they were.

'Well, you've got all weekend to talk. Maybe it'll seem clearer after a good night's sleep.'

'Maybe. And, since the urge to dropout was precipitated by a week's suspension from school, there's no rush.'

'You certainly seem to have your hands full.' *Well, they were big, capable hands and she was rather hoping to fill them herself.* The thought came from nowhere, and Amanda made a determined effort to drag her subconscious back onto the straight and narrow. 'What's she been suspended for?'

'Oh, nothing too dreadful. She dyed her hair.'

'That's all?'

'Not quite.'

Amanda found it disgracefully hard not to laugh when he told her what Sadie had done. The fact that Daniel's mouth was betraying his own amusement didn't help, and her repressed giggle erupted without warning.

'Horrible child,' she said, when she had recovered her breath.

He grinned. 'Do you know, I have the feeling that is exactly what the formidable Miss Garland would have said if she were here?'

'Is that what you think?' She laughed at that, too. In fact she was laughing rather a lot, she noticed. The seminar might have been dull but in every other way the day was turning out very well indeed. 'I can see I shall have to be very careful, or I'll become just like her.'

'Sure,' he said. They were stopped at traffic lights and he turned on the full force of that killer smile. 'When shrimps learn to whistle.'

'Er, excuse me? Was that supposed to be compliment?'

'Well, you know Miss Garland. What would you say?'

Any number of things, Amanda thought, none of them what he expected. But why risk spoiling things? 'I'd say, I've had a boring day and you've had a fretful one. Why don't we stop somewhere and I'll treat us both to a cup of coffee and a sticky bun as a treat?'

Daniel didn't answer, and for a moment she thought perhaps she'd gone too far. Then he signalled a left turn and pulled onto the forecourt of one of those bright, cheerful little restaurants that provide coffee and comfort food twenty-four hours a day for busy travellers. Only then did he turn to her. 'Was this what you had in mind?'

'What do you do for an encore?'

'Sorry?'

'After the mind-reading trick.'

'If I could read minds I'd know what to do about Sadie,' he said as he opened the door for her.

If you could read minds, Amanda thought, I'd be in big trouble.

She picked up a tray, but Daniel took it from her. 'I dare say you've been running about with cups of tea for spoilt executives all day. Go and sit down. I'll get the coffee.'

'Garland Girls don't make coffee,' she said, surrendering the tray but following him along the counter. Then added, straight-faced, 'Well, not unless it's Jamaica Blue Mountain.'

He stopped by the self-service capuccino. 'You're sure you want to risk this?'

She put a mug beneath the spout and pressed the button. 'This is fine. It just needs a good slosh of chocolate powder.' She repeated the process. 'And now we need a truly sticky bun,' she said crisply. 'What about those?'

He looked at an array of Danish pastries. 'Was your day that bad?'

Her day had been something of a roller-coaster ride. At the moment she was on top, but she was well aware that the next half an hour could take it either way. Or maybe she was just kidding herself. 'Actually, on second thoughts, nothing could be that bad. But you go ahead.'

'The coffee will do just fine.' He insisted on paying for it and carried the tray to a table.

They sat opposite one another, and for a moment neither of them said anything. Amanda realised she had started something she didn't know quite how to finish.

Daniel stirred his coffee. 'I was wondering,' he said, after a moment. 'About those tickets—'

From somewhere near her feet, Amanda's mobile phone began to ring. She ignored it. 'Tickets?' she prompted.

The phone continued to trill urgently. 'Hadn't you better answer that?'

Amanda sent a silent message to whatever gremlin was in charge of messing up the communication networks. He was out. And the phone kept on ringing. She retrieved it from her bag. 'Yes?'

'Amanda, where are you? you've got to come back to the office!' Beth sounded like an over-excited puppy.

She was horribly conscious of Daniel, watching her. 'What's happened?'

'I been talking to Guy Dymoke!'

Guy Dymoke? 'Do you mean Guy Dymoke the actor?'

'Actor?' Beth's voice rose several octaves. 'I've never noticed whether he can act. The man is sex on legs—'

'And?' Amanda interrupted before the woman passed out from excitment.

'And he's shooting a new movie in London. He needs a secretary, sweetie, and he wants one of our girls.'

Amanda glanced at Daniel, who was trying not to look too interested. 'Can't you handle it?'

'Are you kidding? He wants to talk to the boss.'

'When?'

'Right now. He's at Brown's Hotel. How soon can you get there?'

Amanda looked at Daniel. The honeyed cowlick of hair. The haze-blue eyes. The roller-coaster hit downhill. 'Hold on.' She pressed the secrecy button. 'Daniel, I'm sorry, but I need to get to Brown's Hotel as quickly as possible. How long will it take?'

Like riding a bicycle, eh? Daniel had been running on instinct with Mandy Fleming, ignoring every rule in the book. What on earth had he been thinking of?

If he ever found out that one of his drivers had done something like this the man would be out on his ear.

And then Mandy's phone had rung and he'd been off the hook.

At least that was what he kept telling himself after he'd dropped her off in Albemarle Street to meet the one man in the world just about any woman would give her right arm to be sharing a hotel suite with. Even if she was just taking shorthand notes.

CHAPTER THREE

'AND the earliest available date that the clinic could manage was in November.' Having dragged every last detail of her meeting with Guy Dymoke out of her, Beth was finally bringing Amanda up to date on last Friday's calls.

'November?' Amanda wanted a child of her own and she knew this was the sensible, rational way to go about it. So why, suddenly, did it seem so cold-blooded, so heartless? How would they go about it? Would they give her a check-list of features she wanted in her donor—six foot three, shoulders just *so* big, eyes like heat haze on a summer day… 'November is fine. There's no mad rush.'

'Oh? Have you been reading all those child-rearing books and gone off the idea?'

'Of course not.' Well, not exactly. But she had spent the weekend thinking about watching her baby grow and wondering where that dimple had come from, or why his hair fell in a cowlick over his forehead. About living with the fact that she'd never be able to say *You're just like your father…*

'Are you sure there were no other messages?'

'No. Were you expecting one?'

'Yes… No…' She caught Beth's eye. 'Well, maybe.'

Daniel opened his desk drawer and the pale jade earring seemed to wink at him, encouraging him to pick up the phone and call the Garland Agency. Instead he reached for an envelope, wrote Mandy's name on it. He'd drop it in their letterbox tonight. It was the sensible thing to do.

'Okay. Tell me all about him.'

'Who?'

'The guy who hasn't phoned.'

'He's no one you know.' Beth just grinned and Amanda felt herself going rather warm. 'I met him on Friday.'

'And?'

There was no point in beating about the bush. 'I think he might be quite perfect.'

'A perfect man? Darling, there's no such animal.'

'It depends what you want the animal for.' And this time she did blush.

It took a moment for the penny to drop, but when it did Beth grinned broadly. 'Oh, I *see.* That's why you weren't bothered about the waiting list at the clinic. You've found your own personal sperm bank and you're planning on making a withdrawal. What's his name?'

Well, it wasn't a State secret. 'Daniel Redford.'

'Nice name.' Beth straightened from her chair and crossed to the coffee pot. 'Want some?' she offered, picking up the pot.

'No, thanks. I'm on a pre-pregnancy diet.'

'Oh? Since when?'

'Since I met Daniel Redford.'

'I do like a woman who knows her mind.' Beth poured herself a cup of coffee, added cream and sugar, then, cradling the steaming cup between her fingers, she leaned back against the table and regarded her boss thoughtfully. 'Lust at first sight, was it?' She didn't wait for a reply. 'Well, it has to be. I suppose he was at the seminar? Well, you don't waste time, Amanda, I'll give you that. Once you see something you want, you go for it.' She sipped her coffee.

'And how does Daniel Redford feel about being the father of your child?'

'I haven't asked him.' She pulled absently on one of the long amber earrings she was wearing. 'Maybe I'm just kidding myself.' She'd hoped he would have called and left a message on the office answering machine over the weekend. She'd checked it half a dozen times. Maybe he'd changed his mind about… well, whatever it was he'd been about to say about tickets when Beth's call had interrupted them.

He'd scarcely spoken to her on the mad dash into London. Of course he'd been edging the speed limit all the way. Conversation would have been distracting.

Or maybe he'd already been regretting the impulse that had prompted that coffee stop. He'd undoubtedly get into deep trouble if his boss found out about it.

She'd considered giving him the number of her mobile phone, writing it down on a piece of paper and saying, *Call me.* But when it had come to it, she'd lost her nerve.

'Perhaps he was just indulging in a mild flirtation over the employment statistics,' Beth offered. 'He's probably married with half a dozen children.'

'Divorced with a teenage daughter.'

'Yes, well, I suppose any man old enough to interest you would have to have been married at least once. Why don't you call him? Ask him to dinner? Tell him you have a proposition to put to him, a business proposition. You never know, he might actually jump at the chance.'

'You could have put that more tactfully.'

'Think about it. I don't doubt that he'd be eager to leap into bed with you at the first opportunity. I'm not so sure he'd want to father your offspring. Babies are expensive.'

'But I don't want his money. I don't want anything from him.'

'Apart from his DNA? I know that. But he might find it hard to believe. Who is he, exactly?'

'Exactly? He's the driver of the car that took me to The Beeches.'

'Oh.' Beth appeared genuinely stunned. 'Oh.' Then, 'He flirted with you, didn't he?' She laughed. 'Flirted with the great Amanda Garland!'

'Yes. At least…' She didn't understand why he hadn't phoned. Of course, she could have misread the signals; it was a long time since she'd dated someone she hadn't met through friends or family or business. A long time since she'd dated anyone who'd inspired the breathless catch of excitment that even now, thinking about him, made her pulse quicken. Someone should have phoned.

Beth's laughter broke into her thoughts. 'Well, I'll give the man ten out of ten for courage. Had he any idea what he was doing?' Her eyes were lit up now, eager to hear it all.

But Amanda wasn't ready to admit to that excitment. 'None whatever. In fact, he was less than polite about Amanda Garland. He seems to be under the impression that she's an old battleaxe—'

'Priceless! What did he say when you told him?'

'I didn't. Tell him. I told him my name is Mandy

Fleming.' Beth's eyes widened. 'Well, it is.' Then, because she didn't want to talk about it any more, she firmly changed the subject.

Maybe it was a bad idea just putting the earring in an envelope and dropping it through the letterbox. It might get lost. Daniel reached for the phone. Maybe, if he waited, she'd phone. While he hesitated, it rang. He snatched it up. 'Yes?'

'Lady Gilbert's here to talk about her daughter's wedding.'

'Oh. Yes. I'll be right there.' He screwed up the envelope and tossed it into the bin. On the point of putting the jade earring back into his desk drawer, he dropped it into his pocket instead.

Beth didn't let it rest. She answered all Amanda's queries about childcare and employment law, then returned to the more interesting subject of Daniel Redford. 'Are you telling me that this guy thinks you're one of your own temps?' Receiving no reply, she shook her head. 'That sounds like trouble.'

'Probably.'

'Oh, dear. He's a bit of a toe-tingler, is he?' *Toes, knees, everything.* She didn't deny it, just stared at the telephone. *Ring, damn you!* The phone rang and she snatched it up. It was her brother, asking her to lunch on Sunday.

'Tell me about him,' Beth continued, as if they hadn't been interrupted.

'He's about forty, I suppose. Something of a rough diamond. He has nice eyes,' she said, remembering, and smiling as she remembered. 'They sort of crinkle up at the corners…'

'Oh, I like the sound of that…'

'And his mouth…' She couldn't get his mouth out of her head. Or the way the whole of his face took part when he smiled, the feel of his hand beneath hers. 'He has lovely hands. Big.' She was beginning to have daydreams about those hands, the way they would hold a woman, or a baby and never let them go. 'Not soft, you know?'

'I'm beginning to get the picture. Would you like to borrow a cookery book?'

'Mmm?'

'You'll want to cook something special,' Beth said, slowly and carefully, as if to someone not quite in possession of all her faculties. 'Just don't forget the whipped cream. It comes in aerosol cans. Handy if he fancies you for dessert…'

Amanda allowed herself to dwell on the image Beth evoked for about thirty seconds. 'No. Forget it. I'm crazy to even think about getting involved with a man for this. You're right, it's just asking for trouble.'

'I didn't say it wouldn't be fun, though. If you're going to do something crazy I don't see why you can't go the whole hog and enjoy yourself at the same time.'

'It wouldn't be fair on Daniel. I'd be using him.'

'I'm sure you'd see to it that he had a good time.' Beth could be maddeningly frank at times.

'That's not the point,' Amanda snapped. 'Besides, I'm not crazy. Do you realise that the birth rate in this country has fallen to a dangerously low level? Forget two point four children, it's down to one point eight. That's below replacement level. Demographic suicide.'

'I'm *so* sorry,' Beth said, deeply sarcastic. 'You're just doing your bit for Queen and country. And there was me thinking you were suffering an acute case of broodiness because your sister-in-law is glowing with mid-pregnancy bloom.' She didn't deny it. She might, just possibly, be crazy, but she wasn't self-delusional. Beth shook her head. 'You are crazy, you know. You've got a private income that would rival the national product of a small country, you run the top secretarial agency in London, and when you're not being a high-powered businesswoman you're at some glamorous premiére on the arm of one of the great and good, or spending the weekend at a country estate—'

'Because I've nothing to stay at home for. It's all a bit shallow. A bit self-centred, don't you think?'

'It sounds pretty good to me.'

'But what about when I'm forty? Or fifty?' Beth remained silent. 'This isn't a spur of the moment decision.' She shrugged. 'All right. I'll admit that Jilly's pregnancy may have set off the alarm on my own biological clock, but maybe it needed a wake-up call.'

'Then do it properly. Get married, make a family.'

'It's not that easy.' She shrugged again. 'Or maybe I'm just too fussy. When you get to thirty you're less able to put up with other people's little foibles, you see all the disadvantages too clearly.'

'Well, you know what I always say. What you lose on the foibles you gain on having someone to warm your feet on at night.'

Amanda laughed, obligingly, but the sound was hollow in her ears. 'It's easy for you, Beth. You fall in love at the drop of a hat. But it's just never happened to me. Maybe I've been too busy all my life for romance; my mistake, but I've left it too late for that.'

'It's never too late to fall in love with the right man.'

'Only an incurable romantic would believe that.'

'Your brother seems to have found the secret.'

'Max and Jilly...' she began. Then her face softened. 'Max and Jilly *are* incurable romantics. The rest of us know that it's just chemistry. One in every three marriages ends in divorce, with the woman left to bring up the children on her own. I'm simply cutting out the middle man.'

'You're cutting out the man altogether.' Amanda said nothing. 'Cutting out the emotion, cutting out the sharing, cutting out the love. Have you any idea what that will be like?' Amanda hadn't thought that far ahead. Didn't want to. 'Women need more. You're heading for trouble, Amanda.'

'What I'm heading for is motherhood. And I have my heart set on a baby boy with blue eyes...'

'That crinkle in the corners?' Beth completed for her. 'Okay. Point taken. But if you're going for it, you might as well have something to remember during the long, lonely, sleepless nights. Men are programmed to scatter their seed indiscriminately, you know. I've been led to believe that they actually quite enjoy it. It wouldn't hurt to give him a call.'

'And ask him, you mean?'

'You haven't been listening, Amanda. First the bait, then the hook. Get to know him first, then...' Beth's hands made vague winding up motions '...then you ask him.'

'And if he says no?'

'You'll know by then what the answer is likely to

be. If it's likely to be no… Well, you say he thinks that you're Mandy Fleming, temporary secretary?'

'So?'

'Maybe you should leave it like that. He need never know that you're Amanda Garland.'

Amanda was scandalised. 'Beth, are you suggesting what I think you're suggesting?'

'Need he?'

'You're suggesting I just… help myself?'

Beth began to giggle. 'Call it a bank raid,' she said, then hooted with laughter. 'A stick-up…'

'Beth!'

'A hold-up!' she gasped.

'Go away, Beth.'

But Beth had collapsed helplessly into a chair. 'Oh, this is just too funny…'

'No, it isn't,' Amanda said, through tightly gritted teeth.

'No. No, you're right. I'm sorry.' She mopped her eyes, cleared her throat, made a determined effort to keep her face straight. 'It isn't funny at all. It's crazy.' She was suddenly deadly serious. 'Are you sure I can't get you a cup of coffee? A brandy, even? Perhaps you should go and lie down in a darkened room—'

Amanda shook her head. 'I told you, no coffee. No alcohol, either. And you'd better see about installing a fridge in here. Somewhere to keep milk and fresh orange juice.'

'The appointment at the clinic isn't for weeks. Of course in the meantime…'

In the meantime Daniel might phone.

Beth was looked up at the ceiling, as if for inspiration. Finding none, she shrugged. 'I know I'm going to regret encouraging you. I know you're going to regret me encouraging you. You'll probably fire me the minute you discover the test shows positive...'

'I won't be able to do that. Expansion means I'm going to need a partner. Someone to share to burden. I thought you might fancy the job.'

'You want me to be your partner? Amanda...' Beth opened her mouth, closed it again. 'I don't know what to say.'

'They do say that there's a first time for everything. Unless, of course, you're still questioning my judgement?'

'As if I would.' Beth's smile was so wide her mouth was practically touching her ears. 'You clearly know exactly what you're doing. I'm sure that you and Daniel Redford will make the most beautiful babies.'

'I thought we'd decided that was a non-starter.'

'Really? And I thought we'd decided that he'd be a lot more fun than a syringe in a clinic.'

Amanda had been trying very hard not to think about that, to bring her imagination to heel. Her imagination however, was playing hard to get. 'And I can tell by the soppy look on your face that you wouldn't have to lie back, grit your teeth and think of England.'

'Probably not.' Her midriff was joining her imagination and turning cartwheels at the thought.

'In the meantime I'll run a check on him.'

The romantic Beth had suddenly turned back into her business manager. 'A check on Daniel? Why?'

'Well, call me cynical, but I don't suppose you're the only woman in the world to have noticed his killer smile and those crinkly baby blues. You've no idea what he gets up to in the privacy of his limousine...

He might be seducing lady passengers all over the country.'

'No, Beth. Absolutely not.'

'Be sensible. Short of asking the man to take a blood test...'

'That's something you put your boyfriends through, is it?'

'I'm not planning on having a baby with a man I've only just met.'

Amanda knew she was protesting because she didn't want to hear anything bad about Daniel. That was every bit as telling as the eager throb of her pulse, the slow heat building low in her belly as she anticipated putting the baby plan into action.

'If it comes to that...' *What?* 'I'll think about it.' Beth didn't look convinced. 'I will.'

After a moment her new partner shrugged. 'Right. Then let's get down to business.'

'I've already started drawing up a partnership agreement—'

'Concentrate! I meant the baby business. You won't be able to ask him to dinner.'

'Why not?'

'Because it wouldn't take him more than two minutes in your Knightsbridge mews to work out that you're nobody's temp, *Mandy Fleming*.'

'I suppose not. But I'll have to tell him—'

'Why? If he's got the wrong end of the stick why put him right? Believe me, a lot of men can't handle a woman who's made it on her own.'

'He's not that small-minded.'

'No?' Beth was still wearing her business manager expression. 'Maybe not. But there is always the danger that your rough diamond chauffeur might just look around at your antiques and your pictures, take in the weight of your silver cutlery and decide that he's fallen on his feet.'

'You don't know him.'

'No. That's why I'm thinking with my head, rather than my hormones.'

'Leave it, Beth. I mean it.'

'Where's Sadie?' Daniel looked around the garage.

Bob slid out from beneath the vintage Bentley that was used for weddings. 'She's gone to lunch with a couple of the lads.'

'Which lads?'

'David, Michael.'

'Ned Gresham?'

'Don't fuss, boss. They know the score.' Dan sincerely hoped so. Particularly Ned Gresham. He'd nearly had a fit when he'd discovered that it hadn't been his secretary, but the local Casanova who'd taken Sadie home on Friday night. 'She's doing fine.'

That was a matter of opinion. 'Not giving you any trouble?'

'She's a bit free with her language, but since she's just trying to shock me I figure it's best to ignore it. She doesn't like cleaning cars, but she knows a surprising amount about how they work. Is she going back to school next week?'

'That's still the plan. Working her way up from the bottom isn't exactly what I had in mind for her.'

Bob got to his feet, wiped his hands on a rag. 'You did it.'

'I had no choice.'

'Yes, well, I wouldn't worry your head about it. It'll all sort itself out in the wash.' There was more coming. Dan waited. 'Sadie was moaning about having to get the bus in to work. Is that part of the plan, too?'

'She can have a lift back to school any time she likes.'

'Point taken. But I was thinking, I've got this little motorbike at home. Nothing fancy. Needs a bit of work. She's got a licence, she was telling me.'

'A motorcycle licence?'

'She said you taught her to ride at the cottage a couple of years ago.'

'I taught her to drive a car too, but she's not old enough for a licence.'

'It's sixteen for a motorbike. She took the test back in the summer when she was staying with one of her friends.'

'Devious little minx. Have you told her? About your motorbike?'

'I only suggested she might like to give me a hand stripping it down one night, after work. Maggie was asking after her. She hasn't seen her for a while.'

'Well, I'll ask Sadie to call round and say hello, but no motorbike, Bob. I don't want her thinking this is some kind of treat.'

He'd known Bob for a long time; he and Maggie had been good friends when Vickie had disappeared, leaving her little girl behind. He hadn't known which way to turn for the best until Sadie had taken things into her own hands and demanded to go to a boarding school. At the time it had seemed like an answer to all his problems. By the time he'd thought about it, worked out that she was simply taking herself away from the possibility of being hurt again, she'd settled in, seemed happy enough.

Daniel took the tickets out of his desk drawer and laid them on his blotter beside the booking slip for the Garland Agency job. Beside the jade earring he'd found in the Jaguar.

Common sense might be telling him that with Sadie going through some kind of crisis it was not the moment to get involved with Mandy Fleming, even supposing she wanted to get involved with him. What woman who mixed with film stars would want to get involved with a chauffeur?

He knew the sensible thing would be to give the tickets to Bob, or someone in the yard, and the earring to Karen, so that she could send it to the agency asking that it be returned to its owner. But what did common sense know about long legs, about the slender, elegant body of a beautiful woman—he picked up the earring, let it swing for a moment from his fingers—about the delicate curve of a small earlobe glinting with gold and jade? He closed his hand around the earring and, after checking the booking slip, he picked up the phone, punched in the number and asked for Beth.

'Beth Nolan.'

'Beth, I wonder if it would be possible to leave a message for Mandy Fleming?'

There was the slightest pause. 'Mandy Fleming?'

'She's one of your temps.'

'May I ask who's calling?'

'Daniel Redford.'

'I see. Well, Mr Redford, I'm afraid I'm not allowed to take personal messages for the girls.'

He wasn't particularly surprised by that. 'It's not personal…' *not much* '…I'm calling from Capitol

Cars. I think Miss Fleming may have dropped an earring in one of our cars last week.'

'Did she?'

'It looks quite valuable. Perhaps you could ask her to call the office, and if it is hers, then we can arrange to return it to her.'

'Why don't you drop it in at the office? I'll see she gets it.'

Bluff well and truly called. 'I'm afraid I can't do that. It's company policy that it's returned in person. I'll need the lady's signature.'

'How very thorough. In that case, Mr Redford, I suggest you leave it with me and I'll see what I can do for you.'

Amanda was prowling her sitting room. She'd told Beth that she needed to work in the quiet of home on her plans for expansion. What she really wanted to do was call Capitol Cars, and she didn't want Beth to know that she'd brazenly dropped her earring in the Jaguar while Daniel had been retrieving her laptop from the rear seat. It was a little more subtle than thrusting her phone number at him. It wasn't something he could ignore. Or maybe he could. Maybe he just wasn't interested. Maybe the earring had been sucked up by a vacuum cleaner unnoticed. She hoped not; it was a particular favourite. Maybe whoever valeted the cars had just tossed it into a lost property box in the office, waiting for her to claim it.

Maybe she should do that right now and put a end to all this nonsense. She snatched up the receiver, quickly punched the buttons before she could change her mind again.

'Capitol Cars, Karen speaking. Can I help you?'

'I do hope so.' Her throat felt tight. Why? There

was no big deal about enquiring for a lost earring. She breathed slowly. Lowered her shoulders and forced herself to relax. 'I've lost an earring and I'm hoping that I may have dropped it in one of your cars. I've looked everywhere else.' *Liar, liar, pants on fire.*

'Oh, isn't that a bother? I'm always losing the wretched things, and what can you do with one earring? When was this?' she asked, before Amanda could reply.

Easy. A piece of cake. The tension seeped from her as she said, 'Last week. I was picked up from the Garland Agency by Daniel Redford,' she said, just for the pleasure of saying his name.

'Dan? That would have to have been Friday, then.'

Would it? Why? 'Yes, Friday. Could you ask him if he found it? It's jade, you see, a favourite. I'll leave my number—'

'Well, hold on, let me check with him.'

Check? He was there? Suddenly the tension was back.

'Mandy?' She hadn't anticipated…hadn't expected… Oh, Lord, she felt as desperate as a fourteen-year-old with a crush on the football captain. Quite unable to speak. 'Hello?'

'Daniel.' Maybe she was coming down with something, because she had to clear her throat again. 'I thought you'd be working. Driving, that is…'

'Not today.' She could hear something like laughter in his voice. Oh, that smile!

'I…um…I was calling about an earring. I think I may have dropped it in your car.'

'If it's a jade drop, you did. Actually, I called the agency a few minutes ago to leave a message for you.'

He sounded so in control. So why wasn't she? 'That's it.'

'So how can I get it back to you? Shall I leave it at the office when I'm passing?'

'And get the traffic warden in a dither again?' The last thing she wanted was Beth ogling him. Making comments. Besides, he sounded so cool. Maybe he needed a little encouragement. She dismissed the idea out of hand. This was a game and he knew all the moves. Witness the way she was panting to see him again. 'If you left it with your receptionist, I could pick it up from the garage some time,' she countered, fingers firmly crossed.

'No…' He didn't want her walking into the garage, discovering that he wasn't quite who or what she'd thought he was. He had this ridiculous longing to know that he was desired just for himself. Assuming that he wasn't fooling himself, of course. He picked up the tickets. *Here goes nothing.* 'I've got a better idea. I've still got the tickets for that show. If you'd like to see it, I could give you the earring then.'

Too cool by half. Teasing her… 'That's very kind of you, Daniel, but I was sure you'd be taking your daughter.'

'Sadie?' She sensed rather than heard the uncertainty in his voice. 'Sadie's grounded until further notice. Besides, I'd much rather take you.' *There, he'd said it.*

'Really?' Oh, Lord! She blushed at the eagerness in her voice. Fourteen? Had she said a fourteen-year-old with a crush? Nowhere near so cool.

'There's only one problem. It's tomorrow night.'

'That's a problem?'

'It's rather short notice,' he said. 'Maybe you're busy?'

For any other man she would be, but this was too important to play hard to get. Besides, she knew she'd already given herself away. Round one to him, then. 'And miss a chance to see the hottest show in town? Tomorrow night will be fine.'

'Curtain-up is at seven-thirty. Can I pick you up?'

Not from home. Despite her scorn, a little of Beth's cynicism must have rubbed off. And she didn't want him anywhere near the office, either. 'I'm not sure where I'll be.' She was beginning to get the hang of this. 'Why don't you leave my ticket at the box-office and we can meet in the crush bar?'

'Why not?' he said. And Amanda had the strangest feeling that he knew that she was keeping him at a distance until she knew him better. 'At seven, then. We can have a drink first.'

She hung up, catching her lower lip between her teeth in an effort to stop herself from shouting out loud. He'd called her first, left a message at the office. She didn't know why that was so important, but it was. It was. Her phone began to ring. It was Beth. 'So, Mandy Fleming, you left an earring in his car, did you? Good move…'

CHAPTER FOUR

'THE man sounds gorgeous.' Beth had insisted on coming home with Amanda to help her decide what to wear for her first date with Daniel. 'Absolutely oozed sex appeal down the telephone.'

'Rubbish,' she said. 'He's got a perfectly ordinary voice.' A bit deeper than most, perhaps. A bit gravelly. 'What do you think of this?' She held up a pale grey dress and jacket.

'For heaven's sake, you're not going to a tea party at Buckingham Palace. Wear the black. You look fabulous in black. And high heels. Men can't resist them.'

'I don't want him to get the idea I'm going to jump into bed with him on the first date.'

'I thought that was the whole point.'

'You've changed your tune. I thought you were the one advising caution.'

'We can all make mistakes. I think you should enjoy yourself.'

'I can't just, well…you know…' Amanda was beginning to wish she'd never told Beth about Daniel. 'I'll have to get to know him first.' Then, 'Stop looking at me like that!'

'Like what?'

'Grinning. This isn't funny. It's serious. Really serious.'

'You can't just… "you know" …?'

Amanda, who hadn't blushed since her knicker

elastic had let her down at a party when she was eight years old, felt her cheeks begin to burn. She tried to get a grip.

'This is just a getting-to-know-you date. He might never want to see me again. I might never want to see him again—'

'Play your cards right and once might be enough. Are the stockings intentional?'

'I always wear stockings.'

'Black stockings?'

Amanda glared.

Beth shrugged. 'Okay, I just thought I'd ask. Perhaps you're just getting into a stew about where you're going to um…"you know"…'

'What?' Amanda was practically shouting.

'When the time comes. You won't be able to bring him here, will you?' Beth replied, with irritating calm. 'Not unless you want him camping out on your doorstep once he's found out what you've done. I mean, he might not have the same ideas about involvement as you do. And so, just in case he wants to be very involved, you'll have to find some discreet little love-nest where no one knows you. That's all.'

Amanda sank onto the bed and glared at her new partner. 'You're really enjoying this, aren't you?'

'Honestly?'

'Honestly.'

Beth grinned. 'I haven't had so much fun since I discovered whipped cream came in aerosol cans.'

'You're disgusting.' And suddenly Amanda was trying very hard not to grin, too. Nerves. Just nerves. 'And you're fired.'

'You can't fire me. I'm your partner. This is definitely the dress, believe me.'

The dress Beth was holding up was short, black and as sexy as sin. 'I don't know,' she dithered. Dithered? When had she last dithered about anything?

'Darling, this little garment covers enough to leave the man in no doubt that you're a lady, while revealing sufficient to leave him panting for more.' Beth's face was deadpan. 'That was the effect you were striving for?'

Amanda swallowed, but there was no point in being coy about it. 'It's the effect women have been striving for since Eve first discovered a fig tree,' she admitted, taking the dress, slipping it over her head, fastening the loops over the tiny jet buttons with fingers that weren't quite steady. 'Well?'

'Very…' Beth's lips curved in an infuriating little smile.

'Very what?' she demanded, fastening a pair of long jet earrings to her lobes. They brushed against her neck like cool fingers, goosing her flesh. She was so *nervous*!

'Very…*"you know"*…' Beth said, with a wicked little giggle.

Mandy Fleming was late. Daniel fingered the tiny jewel in his pocket and wondered if she was going to stand him up. Maybe it would be better if she did. Life was sufficiently complicated without adding a beautiful and sophisticated woman to the equation. One female at a time was more than enough, especially when one of them was Sadie. Especially when Sadie had looked up from the engine she'd been checking for oil and calmly announced that she was going clubbing.

'Clubbing? On your own? In London?' He'd just

about managed to keep the rising hysteria from his voice.

'I won't be on my own. Annabel invited me—'

Which made his neighbour's daughter the least suitable companion for his daughter that he could imagine. With the possible exception of Ned Gresham. 'Then you'll just have to say no. Apart from overlooking the obvious fact that you're grounded, that you're not going anywhere, you are under-age.'

'Annie said I'd get in, no problem.'

Unfortunately she was right. Sadie would have no trouble convincing anyone she was eighteen, which meant the sooner she was back at school the better. 'Perhaps I should have your date of birth tattooed on your forehead.'

'A tattoo? That would be so cool. Just here…' And she'd drawn a fingertip just above her left eyebrow, leaving a streak of oil behind. 'Very small.' Then she'd laughed, that rich, throaty laugh that reminded him so uncomfortably of her mother in full wind-up mode.

It was then that Bob had stepped in and saved the day, asking Sadie, since she'd be at loose end with her dad going out, if she'd like to give him a hand with his motorbike. Or rather had saved his evening, because if he'd had any doubts about wanting to see Mandy Fleming again, his irritation with Sadie for messing up his date had quickly disabused him of them.

Now, with time to think about it, he wondered if he had been set up and worked over by a double act. He'd told Sadie he was going out, if she'd told Bob… He glanced restlessly at his watch. He'd forgotten what this was like. Ten minutes to curtain-up…

'Daniel.' The bar was packed, and somehow she'd found him without him seeing her approach. He rose quickly to his feet, for a moment lost for words. Staying home and playing the heavy father might have been wiser, but when the choice was between that and an evening in the company of a stunningly beautiful woman, wisdom didn't stand much of a chance. 'I seem to make a habit of keeping you waiting.' Below the high-pitched babble of the crowd, her voice brushed softly against his skin, setting it up like gooseflesh.

'You're worth waiting for.' *Oh, God, he couldn't believe he'd said something so crass.* 'Can I get you a drink?' he added quickly, standing aside to let her sit down, eager to escape to the bar and gather his wits, because face to face with the lady he was forced to acknowledge that from the moment she had climbed into his car there had only ever been one thing on his mind. And, while he might not have the sophistication to get his head around ballet, he was bright enough to know that unchecked testosterone was unlikely to endear him to this fair lady.

Amanda settled herself, trying not to stare at him like some lovestruck teenager. She had been so afraid that the reality would be less than the memory, that she had been fantasising about the way he looked, the way he sounded. He was so different from all those cultured men who were her usual companions. Men who'd had all the danger bred out of them.

She'd described Daniel as a diamond in the rough, but that wasn't quite the case. He wasn't exactly rough. But he wasn't smooth either. Now the unaccustomed thumping of her pulse suggested that, like the oyster, a little grit was all it had taken to jolt the planned and ordered running of her life right off the rails.

'Thank you. An orange juice would be fine.' *She was definitely going to need all the vitamin C she could get.*

She watched him carve his way effortlessly through the crowd, catch the eye of the girl serving at the bar. Yes, well, wearing a pale suit, a midnight-blue shirt, a silk tie so loosely knotted that it was little more than a sop to convention, he would catch the eye of any woman with the requisite number of red blood cells. She was surprised she wasn't having to fight off the competition.

He turned with her drink, saw her watching him and smiled. It was then she knew that she would certainly fight. Men like Daniel Redford were rare.

So why had his wife left him?

Her subconscious had this tiresome habit of chipping in at the most inconvenient moments, but on this occasion she could ignore it with impunity. Tonight was just a date. A little fun without commitment to take it any further than the theatre doorway, where she could, by simply raising one hand, be in a taxi and going home alone. *So why did she have the uneasy feeling that would be so much easier said than done?*

He rejoined her at the small corner table he had managed to hold against all comers, put down her drink and settled on the stool beside her. 'Did you have to work late?'

Small talk. She didn't want small talk. She wanted to touch the corner of his mouth with her lips, feel the warmth of his skin against her cheek.

'Yes,' she said, quickly. *Liar,* her subconscious

chipped in. *You were scared. You're scared now.* 'But that's not why I'm late.' She raised her glass to him, took a sip of juice. 'I'm late because I didn't want you to think you were irresistible.'

Dan's breath caught in his throat. He wanted to take her hand and walk out of the theatre with her… 'No danger of that, although I was afraid I was going to have to cancel this evening.' *Small talk. Stick to small talk.* 'Would you let a sixteen-year-old girl go clubbing? In London? Anywhere?'

'Sadie? That's tricky. I'd have to say no, wouldn't I? I mean I'm a responsible adult.'

'But?'

She shrugged. 'But I remember being sixteen and wanting to do things I wasn't supposed to.'

'And how did you feel about your father when he stopped you?'

'Who said he did?' Her lashes did something magical that put the normal in-and-out task of breathing beyond him. 'I mean, why would you ask when you already knew what the answer would be?'

'In other words, I should thank my lucky stars she's not that bright?'

One of those delicately arched brows rose a notch or two, taking his blood pressure with it. 'I wouldn't do that until you're sure you're the winner. Girls are devious little beasts.'

Dan recalled the feeling he'd had that it had all been a set-up, a ruse to get him to give in about the motorbike. 'You could be right.'

'So, why are you here instead of guarding hearth and home? She's a bit old for a babysitter, isn't she?'

'That depends on the babysitter. Bob—he's worked for…for Capitol Cars for years—saved the day. He asked her to go round for supper with him and his wife and then help him strip down a motorcycle.'

Her eyes widened in disbelief, then she laughed. 'Right. I can see how that would be a real treat.'

'Yes, well, by allowing that much I've more or less committed myself to letting her keep it.'

'Can she ride one?'

'I rather stupidly taught her myself one summer holiday. What I didn't know was that she'd taken a test, got her licence.' The bell rang in the bar for them to take their seats. Daniel finished his drink and stood up. 'As you said, devious.'

The theatre made an ideal first date, Amanda decided as they waited for the show to start. There was all that business of settling into their seats, the programme to be perused, none of it needing much thought, or excessive care to avoid saying the wrong thing.

Then there was the brushing of arms as he settled beside her into a seat that was too small for the comfort of a man of his size. The jostling of knees as they had to let a late-comer by. The casual touching of shoulders as she leaned closer to catch what Daniel was saying above the tuning of the orchestra. Nothing of any significance.

Except that the fine cloth of his jacket brushing against her arm sent a shiver of anticipation to goose her skin, set every nerve-ending jangling. Any sane woman would have retreated, but then any sane woman would have been safely at home rather than masquerading as one of her own employees. She leaned closer.

'What did you say?' She'd heard him plainly

enough, but she wanted him closer, wanted to feel his breath against her cheek, the weight of his shoulder against her. She wanted him. Not when Beth assured her it was safe, but now. Tonight.

He didn't answer and she looked up. What she saw in his eyes did not reassure her. Amanda was used to puppy-like adoration from her escorts, but this man was no puppy. He wouldn't walk to heel on command. Or sit up and beg simply for a smile. Quite suddenly she wasn't so sure that walking away would be so easy. At the end of show. At any time.

The seat was too small; Daniel's skin felt too tight. It was crazy. Hell, he hadn't lived like a monk, but he hadn't felt this kind of urgency, this kind of need, in longer than he cared to remember. He remembered the pleasure. His body was reminding him with every throbbing beat of the life flooding through him. Every sense was alert to the faint, exotic scent of her perfume, the whisper of her hair against his cheek as she leaned closer to hear what he said, to the perfection of skin that he knew would feel like silk beneath the hard pads of his fingers. But he remembered the pain of betrayal, too, and he wasn't sure that he could handle the risk.

Then she looked up at him, her dark pupils promising him that he was not alone, that she felt it too. It was just as well they had met in a public place or right now they'd be ripping off their clothes like a couple of desert wanderers stumbling into an oasis. But it wouldn't be water that they were desperate for.

Then the lights were lowered and there was a moment of stillness as the first soft strains of the overture filled the theatre, and anticipation was heightened by the sense of intimacy as they sat together in the darkness.

Amanda tried to concentrate on the performance, but she found it difficult, too conscious of the man beside her, the scent of him, that combination of fresh cloth, good soap, warm skin that was more sensual than any cologne, every cell in her body straining for his touch, her hand positively aching to be held.

She turned again to glance up at Daniel and discovered that he was watching her, rather than the stage. She should have smiled, looked away. She didn't do either, and that was when he reached for her hand, wrapped it in his own huge paw and held it. Then he turned away to watch the performance. He wasn't supposed to do that! That was what *she* did! Her head snapped round so fast that it almost dislocated her neck. But her hand remained in his.

Her hands were so small. They made him feel big and clumsy but he couldn't let go. He was watching the performance but he couldn't have said what it was about, or what anyone had said, or sung. He was only conscious of the satin skin inside her wrist as it slid beneath his thumb, and that touch winding itself around his mind until it took hold of him and bound him fast.

Amanda stared at the performers, acting and singing their hearts out to entertain her, until gradually she was drawn into the story. But all the time, even when, at the close, her eyes unexpectedly filled with tears, she was acutely conscious of the pressure of his fingers, the seductive intimacy of a caress that could lead a sensible, level-headed woman who knew exactly what she wanted to do all kinds of crazy things.

She should move. Reach for her bag, find a tissue.

She did nothing, and because she was sniffing helplessly as the final curtain descended it was Daniel who—while never taking his hand from hers—reached into his pocket, shook out his own neatly folded handkerchief and passed it to her.

'This is ridiculous,' she said, mopping up the silly tears. 'I'm not usually in the least bit sentimental.'

'Maybe you're hungry.'

'Hungry?'

'Hunger lowers the emotional barriers.'

'Does it?' She dabbed at her eyes, laughing self-consciously. He was joking, wasn't he?

'I haven't a clue, but since I was looking for an opportunity to mention that I know an excellent Italian restaurant quite near here, I thought I'd take a chance that you didn't know either.'

'And I said girls were devious. Will we get a table this late?' she asked.

'I booked one. On the offchance that you liked Italian food.'

'And if I don't?'

He grinned. 'There's the all-night hot dog stand on the Embankment.' It was outside; it was public. He was beginning to think it was the only way he was going to get through the evening without doing something really stupid.

'I'll take the Italian,' Amanda replied, abandoning without a second's hesitation any thought of cutting the evening short at the theatre door. As if there had ever been any question of it. She returned his handkerchief. He gathered her wrap and, her hand still in his, they headed for the exit.

Outside he stopped, finally surrendered her fingers, but only to drape the soft cashmere about her shoulders before raising his hand to summon a black cab. One immediately appeared beside them.

'How did you do that?' Amanda asked as he opened the door for her. 'Is there some special signal between drivers?'

'Could be.' He paused briefly to give the cab driver their destination, then joined her, pulling the door shut behind him. 'Or it could be simply that I asked him to come back for us when he dropped me off here earlier this evening.'

In the chill of the night air, without the heat of his fingers to lull her senses, Amanda was suddenly acutely aware of the signals she had been sending and she shivered.

'Cold?' He made a move to put his arm about her, but she was too old to be saying yes with her body and no with her mouth. And, despite the fact that her body was urging her to throw caution to the winds, she wasn't about to allow her head to join in. Unfortunately she wasn't finding that as easy in practice as in theory. Her only hope was to put some distance between them.

So she shook her head firmly, made a business of fastening her seat belt, keeping him at arm's length before she did something she would be sorry for in the morning. 'How disappointing,' she said, avoiding his eyes. 'I was hoping there was some secret wave you could teach me.'

She knew he was looking at her. Knew, without turning, that his eyes had narrowed at the sudden change in the atmosphere between them. 'I shouldn't think you have much trouble attracting the attention of cruising cabbies.'

'No.' But then she wasn't in the habit of summoning cabs, late at night outside theatres. 'You don't live far, then? If you could take a cab.'

'Not too far.'

Why did that sound as if he was avoiding telling her? Amanda wondered. Because she was guiltily conscious of keeping her own secrets?

'And you?'

It was a perfectly innocent question, but it took her completely by surprise and she said the first thing that came into her head. 'I'm staying with a friend at the moment. In Shepherd's Bush.' Just in case he insisted on seeing her to her door. If he did, and she had to get Beth out of bed to let her in, she would never hear the last of it. But galloping hormones were not the best judge of a man's probity, and this way she couldn't possibly put the baby plan into immediate action. The fact that she might be tempted, that she could calmly acknowledge that she might succumb, made her excuse… well, excusable. 'My place is being decorated. And I'm allergic to the smell of paint. It gives me a headache,' she added. Then stopped. The paint thing was true enough. That she had the decorators in was not, and she had always been a terrible liar. She'd said too much. And not enough. Because, despite all the words, she hadn't answered his question. His expression said as much. Mortified, wishing the floor would open up and swallow her, she said, 'I hope I remembered a key.' She'll murder me if she has to get up to let me in.'

Well, that dealt with any possibility of privacy, Daniel realised, because with Sadie at home he couldn't take her there. He had the feeling that he should be relieved. It was too soon. It was too complicated. So why wasn't he? 'I wouldn't want her to do that.'

'No. Look, perhaps supper isn't such a good idea. It's getting late. I have to work tomorrow, and maybe you should be checking up on your daughter…' She realised she was prattling senselessly and stopped.

'Just in case she's gone on the town after all?' Daniel filled in for her. 'Is that what you would have done?' She didn't reply. 'Then maybe I should,' he murmured, then leaned forward and tapped on the glass partition. 'Pull over, will you?' he asked the driver.

'Daniel?'

'It's been a pleasant evening, Mandy. Thanks for your company.' He got out, handed the cabbie a couple of notes. 'Just tell the driver where you want to go.'

'But…' But he had already closed the door and stepped back. She turned as the cab pulled away from the kerb. He wasn't looking; he was striding away down the street. 'Damn!'

The driver slid the glass partition back. 'Beg pardon, miss…?'

Damn! How could she have been so clumsy. So stupid. So *scared*! She couldn't remember the last time she'd wanted a man like that. Wanted him to touch her, hold her. For just a moment she considered asking the driver to turn around, to go after him. Instead she gave him her address, sat back, clasping her hand around her wrist as if preserving the last lingering traces of Daniel's presence.

Nerves. Stupid nerves. She hadn't been out on that kind of date in years. Didn't know what to expect. Didn't know what he expected. Not that it had stopped her from making it crystal-clear what she thought he expected. And if he did? Did it matter? Wasn't that what she wanted too?

No! Not like that. A quick one-night stand. That would be exactly like going to a sperm bank. Then she shivered. No, it wouldn't. Nothing like. Not one bit. And if he had been beside her at that moment, she wouldn't have hesitated to find out how different.

For the second time that evening she was close to tears, but this time they hurt.

So much for the diversion. She should have stuck to the plan.

'Are you going to work today?'

Daniel, dragged from the depths of a sleep that had eluded him for most of the night, opened one bleary eye and regarded his daughter with disfavour. Did she ever wear anything but black? 'Later,' he said.

'Big night, was it?'

'Not exactly. Is that a cup of tea in your hand, or have you just come to torment me?'

'It's Mrs George's morning. The tea is her idea and she thought you must be feeling under the weather. Since you're still in bed.'

'Mrs George is a candidate for sainthood. If you wish to join her please put it down and shut the door quietly on your way out.'

She placed the cup on the table beside the bed. 'What's this?' He dragged an unwilling eyelid back to awake as Sadie bent to retrieve Mandy's earring from the floor.

He'd found it in his pocket with his keys after a long, head-clearing walk home. Until then he'd been congratulating himself on a narrow escape. He wasn't sure what from, but he'd heard enough lies from Vickie in his time to know when he was being fed garbage. He wasn't going down that street again. No matter how loud his body was protesting.

'It's an earring. Don't they teach you anything at that expensive school?'

Sadie pulled a face. 'Very funny.' She dropped it beside the cup. 'I won't embarrass you by asking what it's doing on your bedroom floor. I'm sure I'm far too young to know.'

That, he doubted. 'It's on my bedroom floor because I dropped it there.'

'Right. But who was wearing it at the time?'

'Sadie, go away.'

'You're not getting up, then? I thought, since you're so late already, you might give me a lift in today. That's if you're not too hung-over to drive?'

'I am never that hung-over. I'm not hung over at all. I simply had a bad night.'

'That's not what the earring says.'

Dan gave up trying to catch up on the sleep, sat up and reached for the tea she'd brought him. 'Sweetheart, if I was going to have that much fun, I promise I wouldn't be doing it with you next door, listening.'

'Bit of screamer, is she?'

He didn't even want to think about that, so he picked up his watch. 'You've got ten minutes to get to work.'

'Or?'

'Or you can take your chances at the Job Centre.'

Amanda arrived late at the office, her dark-ringed eyes hidden behind dark lenses. 'Don't ask,' she warned. 'Not a word.'

'Orange juice? Herb tea?' Beth enquired sweetly.

'Coffee. Strong, black and sweet.'

'I read that too much coffee can make it harder to conceive,' Beth said, placing a cup of camomile tea and a pill in front her.

'Did you? And what's this?'

'Vitamin B6. 10 mg. I read that if you take one of these every day for about a month before you get pregnant it'll help prevent morning sickness.'

'You read too much.'

'And my dad brought you some spinach from his garden. It's in the fridge.'

Amanda's insipient headache, caused by lack of sleep and self-disgust, gave up the unequal struggle to remain a threat and kicked in with a vengeance. 'Spinach? Fridge?'

'You asked me to organise a fridge. It arrived this morning. I've stocked it with orange juice, pasteurised yoghurt and skimmed milk.'

'*Skimmed* milk?'

'Low fat, high calcium.'

'Skimmed milk and spinach,' Amanda repeated weakly. She felt sick already and she was nowhere near pregnant.

'I've been reading your diet sheet. You should be eating lots of leafy vegetables.'

Amanda shuddered and changed the subject. 'I was expecting the lease for the ground floor to be biked over this morning for signing. Has it arrived?' she enquired.

'Take off your dark glasses and you'll see that it's in front of you. What happened? Heavy night?'

'Nothing happened. I didn't sleep, that's all.' Then, realising that her remark was open to more than one interpretation, she added, 'We parted after we left the theatre. End of conversation.' She sipped the tea, pulled a face, opened the lease and began to read. After a moment she pressed her hand against her throbbing forehead. 'I need some paracetamol.'

'You need lavender. Try this.' Amanda looked at the small glass vial Beth offered with disbelief. 'It's aromatherapy balm. You rub it on the pulse-points. It'll make you feel much better.'

'I don't need New Age magic drops for that, Beth. I need a painkiller,' Amanda replied, through gritted teeth. 'Now.'

CHAPTER FIVE

'I TAKE it the baby plan is on hold, then?'

'Which baby plan?' Amanda snapped, then winced.

'Try the lavender.'

Amanda removed her glasses in order to glare at her new partner. 'You are in serious danger of irritating me, Beth.'

'Who else would dare?'

Amanda, despite the headache, found her anger seeping away as she responded to a smile. It was herself she was angry with, for allowing herself to be suckered into something that common sense had warned her was a mistake. And then not having the courage to follow through.

'Oh, go on, then. I'll give it a try.' She took the lavender, applied it generously to her throat and temples.

'Wrists too. Then you hold them to your face and breathe deeply. So, what happened?'

'Nothing. We met in the crush bar. The show was lovely. He asked if I'd like to eat Italian and I said yes. Then, in the taxi, I found myself babbling about how I was staying with a friend in Shepherd's Bush…'

'In case he got heavy?'

'In case I did.'

'Ooohhh.'

Slow, drawn out, thoughtful, there was a world of meaning in that little word, and Amanda hid her face behind her wrists and breathed deeply. Actually it was wonderfully soothing.

'And?' Beth demanded.

'Then I realised he'd got the message in a big way and so I said it before he did.'

'What?' Beth plumped herself down on the chair opposite her, elbows on the desk, her face propped in her hands. Immovable until fed large quantities of juicy gossip. 'What did you say?'

Amanda shrugged. 'That perhaps it was a bit late. That I had work in the morning, that he had his daughter to check up on… She wanted to go clubbing, you know. In London. She's only sixteen…'

'You mean you ran scared.'

'I didn't expect him to take me up on it without an argument!' she declared furiously.

'A man capable of surprising you? Well, there's a novelty. What did he do?'

'Stopped the cab, thanked me for a pleasant evening and said goodnight.' She still couldn't believe the nerve of the man. He could have given her a second chance. Everyone knew that men didn't know when no meant no. So how was it she'd got lucky?

'Sheesh. Cool, or what?'

'Or what,' she replied snappishly. 'Cheap, even. He'd been given the tickets and I guess he's not the kind of man who buys dinner for a woman who isn't prepared to respond with a bed for the night.'

'You don't believe that.'

'Don't I?'

'If you believed that you wouldn't be this mad. I have simply got to meet this man.'

'It's easy. Hire a car. I'm sure he flirts with all his passengers.' Amanda groaned. Of course she didn't believe it. It would be a whole lot easier if she did. 'You're right, of course. He gave the cabbie a handful of money to take me home. Didn't even ask where.'

'In other words he just thought you were uncomfortable with the way things were going and stepped back?'

'Behaving like a real old-fashioned Sir Galahad? Get real, Beth. He was offended, thought I was a tease.'

'Were you?'

'I don't know! Maybe.' Beth raised her brows a fraction. 'All right. Yes. I was sitting there, all through the damned show, just waiting for it to finish, desperate for it to finish. But all it took was a dose of cool night air to bring me to my senses. I told you, I'm getting too old for these games.'

'So ring him. Apologise.'

'Apologise!'

'I realise that when you're perfect you don't have to use the words very often, but it's not difficult. Humiliating, but not difficult. You say ''I'm sorry I was so stupid''... Heck, tell him the truth; he'll be flattered...'

Amanda glared at her, but Beth was unperturbed.

'And then you invite him round for supper at this flat in Shepherd's Bush that he thinks you made up. That'll fix him.'

'But I did make it up.'

'Don't be so hard on yourself. There is a friend, and there is a flat.'

'And what if he says yes?'

Beth's grin could have taken in a banana, sideways. 'I'll shift the dust bunnies from under the bed, put on my best sheets and go and stay at your place for the night. Or maybe I'll even give Mike a treat and stop over in the tip he calls home.'

'You should get a place together.'

'He's not housetrained, and until he is he can live with his own ring around the bath.'

'Thanks, but no thanks.' She should have gone with her instincts while she had the chance. If it had been a business proposition she wouldn't have hesitated. She always trusted her judgement when it came to business. Personal relationships had never been so easy.

'You're not going to give up on him, are you? On those crinkly eyes? That dreamy smile?' Amanda did not respond. 'You've never given up on anything you wanted in your life.'

Amanda shook her head. 'He's the stubborn kind, Beth, he won't call again.'

'So, forget your pride and call him. Leave a message at the garage.' She picked up the telephone, punched in the number, offered the receiver to Amanda. 'Ask him to supper. Tell him your friend is away for the night.'

'I can't do that!'

'Capitol Cars. How can I help you?'

Beth covered the speaker with her hand. 'Of course you can. In fact it's a great idea. You needed somewhere to…"you know"…'

Amanda blushed, but she didn't say no.

'Hello, Capitol Cars.'

Beth put the receiver into her hand.

'Capitol Cars, can I help you?'

She looked at it helplessly.

'Speak,' Beth hissed.

'Hello?'

'Now!'

'Uh, Good morning. This is… This is Mandy Fleming. Is it possible to speak to Daniel Redford?'

'Good morning, Miss Fleming. Did you get your earring back?'

'My earring?' *Her earring!* He still had her earring. 'No. No, I didn't. That's why I'm calling,' she said, snatching at straws. 'Daniel was going to return it, but he hasn't got around to it yet.'

'Well, he's just come in…' *Late, like her? Or had he been out already?* 'If you'll hold on, I'll ask him about it.'

'No, don't do that,' she countered quickly. A cool brush-off on the telephone would be just too easy. She'd done it herself on more occasions than she cared to remember. 'I'm passing the garage this morning; I'll call in. Will he be there in about an hour?'

'He's not going anywhere before lunch.'

'There, that wasn't so difficult, was it?' Beth said soothingly as she took the receiver and replaced in on the cradle.

Amanda simply stared at her, then at the lavender balm. 'That stuff is dangerous,' she said, standing up, picking up her bag. 'And you are a bad influence on me.'

'Anything to oblige. Where are you going?'

'To collect my earring. And maybe, just maybe, ask the man to supper.'

'It's not going to take you an hour to get there.'

'I know. But if that girl tells him I'm on my way, he might decide to beat a hasty retreat.' She slipped on her dark glasses. 'This way I'll cut him off at the pass.'

'That's my girl.'

* * *

'Karen, will you put this in an envelope with a compliment slip?' Daniel dropped Mandy's earring on her desk. 'Send it to Mandy Fleming at the Garland Secretarial Agency. You've got the address somewhere.' It was what he should have done in the first place.

'I was going to ask you about that. Miss Fleming phoned just now. She's coming over to pick it up.'

'She's coming here?' Daniel felt his skin tighten, the tempo of his pulse pick up a beat. At a distance, by post, it was easy to be cool. Face to face… 'When?'

'In about an hour,' she said, picking up the earring, admiring it. 'This is lovely. And expensive. I can understand why she wants it back. Don't worry, I'll see she gets it.'

'Yes.' That would be the wisest thing to do. The sensible thing. 'No, wait.' He took it from her. 'I really should apologise for the delay.'

He would have her shown into his office, enjoy the spectacle of seeing her fall over herself to be nice, trying to persuade him that she wasn't a tease once she realised that all this belonged to him. Then he would have great pleasure in showing her to the door. Good God, it wasn't as if he was a kid. He was old enough to take a woman out without expecting her to go to bed with him. Old enough to take her there with all due precautions if they agreed it would be a mutually enjoyable experience. Just because he hadn't been able to think of anything else since she'd stepped into his car, that didn't mean he was going to jump her. Or was he kidding himself? Had she seen the hot need in his eyes and bailed out while she still could?

'Show her in when she arrives.'

Karen grinned. 'I remember now. She was the pretty one, wasn't she?'

Since she was on her way to the office right now, there was no point in denying it. 'Yes, Karen. She was the pretty one.'

'Shall I book a table for lunch somewhere expensive?'

'That won't be necessary.'

'Pity.'

Yes. But there it was. And a man with a teenage daughter who had dangerous ideas about going clubbing would be more sensibly occupied staying at home and keeping her in line than wasting time chasing rainbows.

'Boss?' Daniel was checking the huge wall planner that covered one wall of his office. Not that it needed checking. But he had to do something to avoid thinking about Mandy Fleming. Something that required total concentration.

'What is it?' he asked, without turning around. The concentration bit was difficult enough without interruptions. He certainly wasn't in the mood for Sadie being smart.

'The Silver Ghost. Bob says can you come and have a listen? He doesn't like the sound of her.'

He turned, frowning.

'She's booked out for a wedding tomorrow.'

'I'm well aware of that.' The huge vintage Rolls was his pride and joy and he remembered every bride who had ever ridden in her. He glanced at his watch. There was plenty of time before Mandy was due, and checking the Ghost would occupy his mind far more effectively than the wall planner. 'Give me a minute to get into a pair of overalls and I'll be right there.'

'Yes, boss.'

He sighed. Sadie could invest those two words with a depth of sarcasm that had to be heard to be believed.

He was beginning to think that he'd made a serious mistake putting her to work. He'd intended this week to demonstrate to his daughter what life was like in the real world. It was supposed to be a warning. It had seriously backfired, because Sadie appeared to have taken to working for a living with all the enthusiasm of a duckling discovering water.

He would have admired her for that if he hadn't been so certain that she should be back in school, doing those re-sits, working for her A levels. He'd built a company on hard work and single-minded determination and taking the kind of risks that nightmares and broken marriages are made of. Sadie, with a degree in business management, could expand it out of sight if she was that keen.

But Sadie wasn't his only bad decision this week. Maybe he should stop thinking so much and concentrate on the internal combustion engine. That he understood.

He eyed Sadie, sitting at the wheel of the huge car, gentling the throttle. 'Where's Bob?' he asked.

'Call of nature. Listen…'

He shrugged, and listened. There was a faint knocking sound.

'Tappets?' she offered.

He shook his head, watching the beautiful engine as it purred like a contented tiger. Smooth, sleek perfection in motion. Like Mandy Fleming as she'd walked away from him into The Beeches…

'Big end?'

'What? Oh. No.' He dragged his mind back to the job in hand. 'I'd better get underneath and have a look.'

Amanda paid off the taxi and turned to look at the smart frontage of Capitol Cars. Her heart was thumping like a bass drummer on overtime and her mouth was uncomfortably dry. This had to be a seriously bad idea, but since it was the only one she had she might as well get on with it. Taking a deep breath, she pushed open the door.

The woman sitting behind the reception desk in the comfortably furnished office was wearing a tailored suit in the same grey as the one Daniel had been wearing, a small tie-scarf at her throat printed with the company logo. Around the walls were framed photographs of fine cars, a vintage Rolls complete with bride, in pride of place. 'Good morning, madam. How can I help you?'

Amanda recognised the voice from the telephone. 'We spoke about half an hour ago. My name is Mandy Fleming. Is Daniel about?'

The woman smiled. 'Won't you sit down, Miss Fleming? He's in the yard right now; I'll call him for you.'

Give him time to make a quick exit? 'Please, don't disturb yourself. Just point me in the right direction and I'll find him.' She wouldn't expect one of her girls to fall for that, but the telephone began to ring and the woman hesitated. 'I haven't got much time,' she said, adding a little pressure.

'Oh, well. Look, if you go through there and round

to your left you'll find him under the vintage Rolls in the far corner.'

'That one?' Amanda turned to the photograph.

'Yes. We've a wedding tomorrow. Everything has to be perfect.'

'With Daniel driving I'm sure it will be.' *With Daniel sitting in the back it would be better.* 'Through here?' she said, quickly moving towards the door before the frowning receptionist could see the heat that had raced to her face.

'Er, yes…'

She stepped through the door to the rear and into the yard. On the far side there was a long single-storey garage block. There were few cars at home, but those in residence were seriously impressive motors. She walked to the end of the line, turned to the left, and in the workshop she saw the magnificent Rolls. From beneath it protruded a pair of very large feet.

'Sadie, there's something…I can't quite…pass me the inspection lamp, will you?' Amanda looked around. There was no one there but her. The place seemed unusually empty, but it was just about lunchtime. She shrugged, crossed to the workbench and picked up the lamp. 'Come on, girl, I haven't got all day.'

Yes, sir!

A large, oil-smeared hand was waving impatiently in her direction and she bent to place the lamp into it. There was a pause. And then a brief, scatological comment. It seemed as good a moment as any to make his day.

'Is there some problem?' she enquired.

Daniel froze. Then, very slowly, he turned his head

to be confronted not by Sadie's DMs but a pair of very high-heeled, very expensive shoes. Inside the shoes were two slender feet which in turn were supporting a pair of the sexiest ankles he had ever had the pleasure of seeing in such vivid close-up.

The turmoil in his brain was only out-classed by the hot flush of desire that seized him so completely that for a moment he remained where he was while he regained some control of his body, his emotions. Only when he was quite sure that he wouldn't betray himself like an adolescent in hormone overdrive did he push the slider from beneath the car.

Mandy. He had hoped that it might just have been one of those tricks of the mind, like that mirage in a desert he had been thinking about when they were in the theatre. But he wasn't imagining things, and remembering anything about last night was not a great idea. Not when she was leaning over the great curving sweep of the mudguard, looking down at him, the dark glossy wing of her hair falling forward. She reached up, hooked it behind her ear with those long, slender fingers and he knew he was in trouble.

Mandy. Not that he'd needed to see her face. Those ankles had told him everything he needed to know. And her voice. No other voice had ever had quite that effect on him. 'I wasn't expecting you for another twenty minutes.'

'She told you, then? That I was coming?'

'Wasn't she supposed to?'

'I thought you might take an early lunch if you knew.'

'So you came early. Just in case.'

'It's just as well I did, or you'd have had to get

your own inspection lamp.' She glanced around. 'Where is everybody?'

'Down the pub, waiting for me to buy them a drink.' He held out the note that had been wrapped around the little plastic spill responsible for the tapping noise. She took it carefully, avoiding his grease-marked fingers.

'"Gotcha! Sadie",' she read, then looked back to him for an explanation. 'What does it mean?'

'It means I've been had. It's a garage tradition. New boys—or in this case, a new girl—try to catch me out.' He usually allowed himself to fall for it on the third or fourth attempt. When he was sure they would fit into the team. 'Until they do, they're just temporary.' It had never occurred to him that Sadie would try it. What was she trying to prove? That she could outsmart him? Or that she was going to stay?

'After twenty years I suppose you're considered the man to impress?'

He'd planned on impressing her. But not in oil-stained overalls with greasy hands. 'I guess so,' he conceded, finally sitting up, pushing himself to his feet. 'But I've just learned that no one is ever too old or too clever to avoid the well-laid trap. My darling daughter will undoubtedly be beside herself with mirth.'

'I'd better go, then.' She removed the dark glasses that had been hiding her lovely eyes. She hadn't slept so well, either, he noted, but he refused to allow himself to feel sorry for her. 'Since you're so busy.'

'I thought you were going to be busy today, too,' he said.

'My mistake.'

That was all? Her mistake?

'I came by to see if you'd care to take a chance on my cooking. Make up for last night.'

Not quite all, then. And just when he'd been congratulating himself on a very close call. 'Is it much of a risk?'

'Not much of one. I can defrost a TV dinner better than almost anyone I know.'

'That takes talent. What about your friend?'

'Beth?'

'Is that her name?'

'You spoke to her when you rang the office the other day...'

She wanted him to believe in that friend, he thought. Maybe he did, maybe he had got last night all wrong, but she was still hiding something.

'Beth is going out.'

'Really?' He held up his hands. 'Excuse me. I have to clean up.' He started across the yard.

'You still have my earring, Daniel.'

He stopped. That was it. It was the way she said his name. Everyone else just called him Dan or Boss. Even Vickie had never called him Daniel. He turned slowly. She was standing beside the Rolls, looking as if she had been born to sit in the back seat like the lady of the manor, liveried chauffeur up-front. *Well, tough. The chauffeur happened to own that particular car and there was only one way she was ever going to ride in it.*

Shaken that such a thought should cross his mind, he said, 'It's in the office.'

'I'll ask the receptionist for it, then.'

All he had to do was say yes and it would be over. His head was telling him that would be the sensible thing to do; his gut and his heart refused to listen.

This beautiful woman still thought that he was just a driver but she'd come back anyway. It was what he had wanted, to be desired for himself. So why was he holding back? Because he didn't believe in fairies? Or because he knew that this wasn't any minor flirtation. He'd been there, done that. This was different. She was different.

'No. No, don't do that. If you can wait until this evening I'll bring it with me.' He felt exactly like a man who has just stepped out of a plane and is waiting for the parachute to open. Elated, scared witless…

Her smile was worth it. 'I can wait. Is seven too early?'

That long? 'Seven is just fine.' How on earth could his voice sound so controlled when his insides were behaving like a kindergarten class on a day trip to the zoo? 'What's the address?'

She opened her bag, took out a notebook and wrote it on a piece of paper. 'There. And that's my mobile number. Just in case…' Her voice faded away as she raised those long silky lashes and met his gaze head-on. She was so close, her mouth so soft, so inviting. He reached out, stopped his hand an inch short of her cheek, but his mouth kept moving towards her—

'Dad!' He dropped his hand like a guilty child caught with his fingers in the biscuit tin. He'd forgotten all about Sadie. 'We've been waiting for you.' She was standing, arms akimbo, glaring at Mandy.

'I was just coming. Sadie, this is Miss Fleming—'

'Hello, Sadie,' Mandy said, extending her hand.

Sadie kept her hands fastened to her hips. 'The lady with the exotic taste in earrings,' she said dismissively. 'You really shouldn't leave them on the bedroom floor, you know. It's a dead giveaway.' She turned back to him. 'We're in the pub, when you can spare the time.'

He was so angry he wanted to take her by the shoulders and shake her. How dared she be so rude? 'I can't,' he snapped. 'And you're under-age. Bob should know better. Go and get your lunch, Sadie. I'll talk to you later.' For a moment she defied him, before spinning on her heel and walking away. Then he turned back to Mandy. 'I'm sorry. I dropped your earring last night and she leapt to the wrong conclusion.'

'She's at a difficult age,' she said sympathetically.

'Is there an easy one? Look, can I give you a lift somewhere? It'll only take me a minute to clean up.'

She shook her head. 'No, go and make your peace with your daughter. I'll get a cab at the corner.'

At five-thirty Dan went looking for Sadie. 'I'm going home, do you want a lift?'

'No. Thank you.' She was politeness personified, a very bad sign. 'Bob and I are finishing off the bike tonight. Maggie is giving me tea.'

'Again? Don't wear out your welcome,' he said, looking around. 'Where is Bob? His car's not here.'

'He's washing it down,' she said, refusing to meet his gaze. 'He said to tell you that he'd bring me home.'

He could hear the pressure hose working. 'Oh, right.' He flicked open his wallet and took out a note. 'Here, you'd better stop off somewhere and get Maggie some chocolates or flowers.' She took the note, stuffed it into her overall pocket. 'And don't be late. Eleven o'clock. Have you got your key?'

'Having an early night, are you?'

He was finding it difficult to keep his temper, but, since losing it would be giving Sadie exactly what she wanted, an excuse for a row, he tried very hard. 'No, I'm going out to dinner.'

'With the earrings? Doesn't that amount to the same thing?'

'Her name is Mandy Fleming.'

'*Mandy?* You're kidding me?'

'If you don't like it you can call her Miss Fleming. As in ''I'm sorry I'm such an ill-bred brat, Miss Fleming.'''

'Why? Is she going to be a fixture?'

Was she? His body reacted with treacherous enthusiasm to the suggestion, but he ducked the question. 'Have you written to Mrs Warburton yet?'

Sadie's eyes narrowed. Then, after a long moment, she shrugged. 'I did it yesterday.'

'Good.' The stick had got them over one hurdle. Maybe it was time for the carrot. 'Sadie, have you got a crash helmet? A good one?'

Startled, she finally looked up. 'Yes. I bought one out of my allowance. I had to have it before I could take my test.'

He nodded. 'Tell Bob I'll square it with him. About the bike. If you want it.'

He thought, hoped, that he had shaken her out of her sullen mood. But with that deliberately maddening way that teenagers have, she shrugged. 'I'll think about it.'

'Don't strain yourself, Sadie.'

For a moment he thought she was going to keep it up. Then, for the first time all week, it seemed, she grinned. 'Sorry. Thanks, Dad.' Then, her eyes full of mischief that made her look more ten than sixteen, she said, 'Bob said you'd see sense once you had time to think about it.'

'Is that so?' Bowing to the inevitable was more like it, but, since she'd undoubtedly get a motorbike one way or another, he'd like to be sure that it came from a good home. And if he stacked up a few Brownie points against the weekend, when they were going to have to confront the issue of school, so much the better. 'Well, let's hope it runs in the family, eh?'

Chocolates? Flowers? Both? He'd encouraged Sadie to get some for Maggie and now it was his turn. But somehow he doubted that Mandy ever succumbed to the temptation to eat chocolate. Flowers, then. But, glancing at his watch, he realised that it was too late to buy any kind of flowers except the stiff, garish mixed bunches they sold on the forecourt of the local filling station, and they wouldn't do.

Mandy was the kind of woman who should have flowers fresh picked from the garden. At the cottage there would be late, full-blown roses, or a fist full of sunflowers, or perhaps the pale, fragile beauty of Japanese anemones…

He stopped the thought right there. Just what had happened to the man who had been going to invite the lady into his office and embarrass the hell out of her? *Yeah. Sure. Just who did he think he was kidding?*

Amanda was a bundle of nerves. The roux caught and she had to make it again. She broke a glass, which was bad, but not a disaster, and a fingernail, which was both. Then the doorbell rang, and the tub of peppercorns she was opening fell apart in her hands and they scattered like shot over the pale blonde polished floor of Beth's exquisite white and chrome minimalist flat. Dust bunnies, indeed! As if a mote of dust would ever dare infiltrate Beth's home, let alone a whole bunny full of them.

For a moment she was forced to grip the edge of the table simply to stop her hands from shaking, then, catching sight of the clock, she realised with relief that it couldn't possibly be Daniel. It was only ten to seven, and he surely wouldn't arrive until at least ten past. Plenty of time to fix her lipstick, her hair. This had to be Beth stopping by to check that she had everything she needed, that everything was working. That she hadn't taken fright again and bolted.

Not this time. But this time she wasn't putting all the goods in the window either. She'd stepped back a pace, chosen to wear nothing more tempting than a pair of grey wide leg trousers, a simple white blouse that buttoned to a high neck, a pale pink lipstick. Even her earrings were plain pearl studs. This was just going to be dinner…

She looked at the floor and groaned. She was the word for efficiency in London, and yet the prospect of spending the evening with Daniel had reduced her to a gibbering wreck. It would take for ever to chase the wretched things around the floor. Then, as the bell rang again, she let out a slow breath. Beth. Beth would do it while she spent a few minutes making herself look presentable. She kicked off her shoes, not wanting to crush the peppercorns against the lovely floor, and stepped cautiously through them to the front door.

Just how wrong could one woman be?

'Daniel.' Daniel looking absolutely gorgeous in a

dark red twill shirt, pleated chinos, a jacket slung over his shoulder and with a couple of bottles of wine hooked between the fingers of one hand.

Daniel. At least twenty minutes before she had expected him.

'I'm too early,' he said as, without a word, she stepped back to let him in. In the light of the hall he could see that she was flushed. Her sleek, well-groomed hair looked as if she'd been using her fingers to comb it without any great success, and her lips, as they'd parted on his name, were full and sweet, and he didn't know how he was stopping himself from putting his arm about her and taking up where they had left off at the garage.

'No. Come in,' she said, ignoring the fact that he was already inside. Her fingers found their way to her hair, slipped through it as she backed into the kitchen, surreptitiously attempting to finger-comb it into some semblance of order. 'It's fine.'

'I couldn't wait,' he said. He put the wine on the kitchen table. 'I'm sorry, but I just couldn't wait...' Something scrunched beneath his shoes but the only thing on his mind, the only thing that had been on his mind for days, was Mandy.

He couldn't wait. The words were like a magic spell, Amanda felt almost giddy, like the sleeping princess woken by a kiss after a hundred years. All those attentive, polite, restrained young men who had danced to her tune since her coming-out party had left her an emotional virgin. But Daniel... Daniel would never dance to anyone's tune. He had his own rhythm, and she was the one longing for him to take her in his arms and waltz away with her!

And with that realisation Amanda stopped worrying about the fact that she'd bitten off her lipstick, that her hair looked like a bird's nest, that she was flushed and dishevelled, and she did what she'd been longing to do since the moment he had looked down at her in the back of that car. She reached up to take his face between her hands, raised herself onto her toes and she kissed him.

CHAPTER SIX

For the longest moment there was a breathless stillness as she gentled her lips across his.

Daniel, brought almost to his knees by an adolescent eagerness that had swept away the man, the father, thirty-eight years in the single-minded pursuit of success, hadn't meant to be early. And when he had found a place to park more readily than he'd anticipated he'd certainly intended to sit in the car and wait for fifteen minutes. He'd had plenty to occupy his mind.

For all of two minutes he had tried to focus on some way of persuading Sadie that she should return to school. There had to be some way of convincing her.

His mind, however, had refused to co-operate. It had kept straying to the door a little way down the street. The mystery of the woman behind it.

What would she be tonight? The cool, teasing flirt who had ridden in the back of the Mercedes? The slightly flushed young woman who'd ridden beside him in the Jaguar and then, with one phone call, turned into a totally dedicated career woman racing off to take dictation from some masculine sex symbol. God, the jealousy should have warned him then how it would be. Would she be that unexpectedly diffident woman who had turned up at the garage today? Or would there be a repeat of that prickly uncertainty that had wiped out last night.

He hadn't expected this.

This was something else. A kiss that said, *Hello*. And, *I've been waiting for you. Wanting you.* A kiss that gave, but demanded nothing. Sweetly pure and yet putting a rocket under the sinful, straight-to-hell thoughts he'd been having ever since he'd set eyes on her. A kiss that a man would remember in his heart on the day he died.

He held her; that was all. His hands at her elbows, steadying her as she stood on tiptoe and sable lashes swept down so that he couldn't see her eyes, hadn't got a clue to her thoughts. But a streak of flour dusted her flushed cheek, whitened her mussed hair, lending her a touch of vulnerability that she had, until now, kept well hidden beneath the aristocratic cheekbones, the cool poise of a smile that looked out on the world with the confidence of a woman who knew she could have it all and intended to take it.

The certain, blissful knowledge that, right now, all she wanted was him acted like draught of oxygen over the damped-down heat that had lingered in his veins all afternoon. It flared to her touch, the fire racing through him so that he could scarcely catch his breath. He didn't want to be this much out of control; he was too old, had seen too much to ever feel like this. But he closed his eyes, anyway. And when, finally, she drew back just an inch or two, sighed a little, looked up at him with those wide grey eyes, he knew he was grinning like the idiot he was.

'I haven't been kissed like that since I was sixteen,' he said, his voice husky with a need that was hammering through him like an express train, bringing him close to madness.

'Is that good?' she asked seriously, as if it really mattered. 'Or bad?'

His hands slid up her arms, silk over sleek, finely muscled flesh. She was strong, special. He wanted to pull her hard against him, mould her to him and let her decide whether it was good or bad. Instead he took his cue from her and simply brushed the flour from her cheek with the pad of his thumb.

'Good,' he said, his voice thick with everything he wanted to say, wanted to do. 'Very good. And about as bad as it gets.'

Her head tilted to one side a little. 'In what way...bad?' She sounded as uncertain, as bewildered as he was, and he wanted to cradle her, reassure her, tell her that it was okay...that bewildered was just fine. But he didn't know the words so he simply took her face between his hands as if it was some fragile and irreplaceable treasure, cupping it in his palms, his fingers lacing through her hair.

'This way,' he said. Then he lowered his mouth to hers and for a moment he paused there, a millimetre from heaven, making her wait, loving the slightly puzzled crease that had appeared between her brows. She was very still between his hands, scarcely breathing, with only the racing of a pulse at her temple beneath his thumb to betray her. Then, as the heat of expectancy built between them, he saw her eyes darken, understanding smooth her brow, a little cat-like smile tuck the corners of her mouth. It was all the encouragement he needed.

He grazed his lips across hers, a touch, no more, and her lashes fluttered down in a silent gesture of total surrender. And still he made her wait. There was no rush. This was not something he wanted to rush.

A small sound escaped her. A *hurry up*, impatient little sound that squeezed at the heavy drag of need low in his belly. It had been there all afternoon, constantly tugging at his concentration, a heat that even the decidedly chilly atmosphere in the garage that afternoon had been unable to cool.

'Good?' he murmured, teasing her, teasing himself as he rationed out the little touches of his mouth, his tongue, against her lips. Like a dance. A slow, sensuous dance…

'Mmm…' The sound was little more than a sigh. 'Very good.' She nipped at his lower lip. The tip of her tongue joined in the game. 'And very bad.'

'Tell me.' The dance, he decided, was something from an old black and white movie, a sensuous, slightly wicked tango. *Slow, slow…*

'You don't need to be told. You already know.'

He knew that she desperately wanted more, wanted to know him, wanted everything, as she coiled her arms about his neck, parting her lips to him. *Quick…* His pulse was racing out of control, spinning. *Turn…* And for a moment his mouth came down hard on hers to demonstrate just how much he'd learned in the long years since he was sixteen.

Slow… Oh, God. This was too soon. He straightened, caught her wrist. 'Let's get out of here.'

'What!'

She didn't believe it. He wasn't sure he did. 'Where are your shoes?'

She waved, wordlessly, at a pair of low-heeled pumps abandoned in the midst of a major spillage of peppercorns. He grabbed them, dropped them by her feet.

'Jacket?'

'There.'

He turned, saw the fine tweed tailored jacket hanging on a peg and he took it down, fed her arms into it as if she were a child.

'Where are we going?' she asked in total confusion. 'What about dinner?'

'Turn it off.' She was still staring at him as if he was mad, so he did it for her, flipping the oven switches to off.

'My soufflé!' she protested, suddenly coming to her senses. He took her hand and headed for the door. 'I sweated blood,' she declared, grabbing at her bag as she passed the hall table.

'Yeah...' He paused by the door, brushed the flour from her cheek, showed her his fingers. 'I saw.'

'Oh, great!' she gasped, and as he opened the door rubbed her palm across her face, her feet stubbornly planted in the doorway. 'It would be a terrible waste.'

'Stay or go,' he warned. 'It's not going to be eaten.'

Amanda wanted to stay. Last night she had been afraid of this. Afraid of the loss of control over what was happening to her. Afraid that Daniel Redford had robbed her of her senses.

Today she wasn't afraid. Today she knew he had. She'd known it ever since he'd come within a whisker of kissing her, and all afternoon she'd been dreaming of how it would be to have Daniel Redford do a whole lot more than that.

Maybe the wait had made it so special. Maybe that was why he was rushing her out of the flat. Perhaps it was anticipation that put on the gloss, the sparkle, did that thing that was making her feel light-headed and just a little bit crazy. Or maybe it was love. She didn't know, because falling in and out of love at the drop of a hat like Beth was an experience that had somehow passed her by. But it was different from anything that had happened to her before, and, since Daniel seemed to know what he was doing, she would trust him in this.

For a moment Dan thought she was going to say stay, but after a moment, she turned and walked through the door, down the stairs and into the street. He paused only to catch her hand, tuck her arm beneath his, before setting off at a brisk walk.

She kept pace without complaint for about a hundred yards, then looked up at him. 'So? Where are we going?'

'Nowhere in particular.' Just out into the sanity of cool evening air and away from the danger of instant conflagration. He turned to look down at her and, suddenly more sure of himself, slowed his pace a little. 'Just putting some distance between us and a bed. I guess I'm about where you were in that taxi last night, Mandy. Wanting the whole nine yards and knowing that it's too damned soon.'

'Oh. I see.'

That was all? No argument? The realisation of what that meant nearly had him turning back to the flat. 'Talk to me. Tell me about yourself,' he said, before desire got the better of him.

'We could have talked over dinner,' she pointed out.

'Yeah?'

Her mouth twitched into a smile. 'What do you want to know?'

'Anything. Everything. You're a secretary, you love going to the theatre, even ballet, although I promise I won't hold that against you, and you're allergic to the smell of paint. I don't think we got a whole lot further than that.' And he wanted to know it all. 'Start at the beginning.'

'Right at the beginning? It could be a long night.'

'You've got until eleven.'

'Eleven?' She gave him a thoughtful sideways glance. 'Are you on curfew?'

'No, Sadie is. Unfortunately, I have to be there to make certain she sticks to it.' He shrugged. 'Fatherhood is hell.'

Amanda smiled. 'You can't fool me. I know all about fathers; I had one myself. You'd do anything, risk anything for her.' *Her child wouldn't have that.* 'All right, Cinderella, it'll have to be the potted version. Let's see, I'm twenty-nine…' she gave a little shrug '…well, very nearly thirty, to be absolutely honest—'

'I like honest.' Daniel caught and for a moment held the glance she flickered in his direction. Again he had that unsettling notion that she was hiding something from him. 'Does thirty bother you?'

'No, why should it?'

He shrugged. 'Thirty is a landmark. Maturity for a man, but for a woman it's the end of any pretence at youth. Some women I've known would never admit to more than twenty-nine.' His ex-wife was one of them. Sadie was a very public statement that she was considerably older, which he suspected was the reason why she had never been invited to join her mother in the Caribbean during the holidays.

'That's a bit sad, don't you think?' Mandy was looking up at him and he promptly forgot all about Vickie and her insecurities. 'Being thirty doesn't bother me; it's just an exclamation mark in life, a reminder of the things I haven't done…things that I thought I would have done by now.'

'There's still plenty of time.'

'For most things. Not for everything.' He had the feeling that he'd touched a nerve, and it didn't take a genius to figure out what it was. She didn't want to talk about it, though, rattling off her history as if aware that she had somehow betrayed a very private part of herself. 'I was born in Berkshire, went to boarding school, thought I might go to university, but my father needed a secretary…' someone he could dictate his memoirs to during that long last illness '…so I did that until he died.'

'You could have gone later. You still could. A lot of people take a degree late.'

'I know.' She smiled up at him, clearly not bothered about it. 'And if I'd wanted to I would have. I like what I do.'

Temping? 'What about family? Your father's dead, but you have a mother? Brothers and sisters?'

'My mother keeps herself busy with charity work. I have an older brother, Max; he's an economist. He and his new wife, Jilly, are expecting their first child at the end of January.'

Hence the preoccupation about where her own life was going. 'That's it?'

'What else? I've never been married, never lived with anyone.' Never met a man who had come close to making that happen for her. Until now. Bad timing? Or unbelievably good timing?

Too good, perhaps. Why couldn't things ever be simple? Twenty minutes earlier they had been a breath away from bed—that was simple, if you like. Simple lust. Simple sex. Exactly what she wanted.

And then Daniel Redford had got all complicated on her.

'Where do you live?'

Complicated and inquisitive. 'Uh-uh,' she said. 'It's your turn.'

Daniel glanced down at her. Still hiding? But then she wasn't the only one. 'Okay. What do you want to know?'

'Start with the basics, then you can improvise.'

'Okay. I was born thirty-eight years ago in the East End of London,' he began, taking his biographical cue from her. 'My father was a brute and a bully and my mother gave up caring enough to live a couple of days after my tenth birthday.'

She stopped. 'Oh, Daniel, I'm so sorry.'

Her hand covering his was so tender a gesture that it nearly undid him. Instead he pushed on, insisting that they keep walking. 'I stopped going to school somewhere between my fourteenth and fifteenth birthdays,' he said roughly. 'Too busy hustling for a living in the markets and along the docks. I was lucky. I could have ended up in big trouble, but instead I discovered that I had an affinity with the internal combustion engine.'

He hadn't said anything about pain. It was undoubtedly buried deep, but it was there. 'I can see why you're so keen for Sadie not to miss out on her chances.'

'She doesn't have to hustle. This isn't about choice. The fact that she flunked her maths and English GCSEs should have warned me.'

'You think it was deliberate?'

'She got As for both in her mocks. She left it a bit late to start rebelling, but I'm guessing the fact that her mother recently had a baby has a lot to do with it. She doesn't ever talk about the way Vickie left her, so it's easy to be fooled into thinking she doesn't care. Or perhaps easier to hope she doesn't.' He glanced down at her. 'I thought a week in the garage would be enough to put her off hard manual labour as a career.'

'And has it?'

'Not noticeably. She's bright—I thought she'd get bored.'

Amanda laughed at his innocence. 'She's sixteen, Daniel. Putting her in a garage and surrounding her with grown men who I'm sure all make an enormous fuss of her isn't likely to provide her with much of an incentive to go back to school.' She tucked her arm deeper into his. 'They have been making a fuss of her?'

'Well, yes, I suppose they have,' he said, thinking of the way Bob treated her like one of his grandchildren. The way that Ned and Michael and the others bought her chocolate and buns… He suddenly caught on to what she was suggesting. 'But no one would dare—'

'No.' Amanda thought he was right. Very few men would dare defy Daniel Redford. 'But Sadie might. If she's in full-tilt rebellion. She's sixteen, Daniel. I doubt Capitol Cars would sack a good driver or mechanic for having some fun with a girl old enough to say yes. And if they did, they'd be on a hiding to nothing if he brought a case for unfair dismissal.' She stopped, turned into him, forcing him to do the same. 'Where is she tonight?'

'Finishing off the motorbike with Bob. He and Maggie are like family; she's safe with them.' Maybe he should have taken Mandy there too, because cool air, a brisk walk wasn't doing it for him. There was still only one thing on his mind. 'Are you hungry?'

She smiled up at him. 'Yes, I'm hungry, but somehow I don't think the soufflé will have survived.' There was something in that low, throaty voice, trembling on the brink of laughter, that suggested a collapsed soufflé was the last thing she was thinking about. 'What do you suggest?'

'We can't go back to that flat.'

'We could.'

Not unless he took a dip in the Serpentine first.

'I could rustle up a bacon sandwich.' She gave a little shiver. 'It's getting colder.'

He wasn't and he didn't think it was cold that was disturbing her, either. 'Here. We'll eat here.' They'd stopped a few yards from a wine bar.

She put her head to one side. 'You think I can't cook, is that it?'

He bent to brush his lips across her forehead. 'You know exactly what I'm thinking. Which is why we'll eat here.'

He pushed open the door, held it for her, and then sat her at a small table in a quiet corner. He ordered wine and food, and Amanda wasn't doing anything but agree with whatever he suggested so that she could watch him. She missed the touch of him at her side, but sitting opposite him was good too. She enjoyed looking at him.

He had a deep cleft in his chin that seemed to invite the edge of her thumb, and in her mind she could almost see him coming awake at first light, feel the roughness of morning stubble as she touched his face. Her imagination was doing her no favours; a busy wine bar was not the place to be having those kind of thoughts, but it wasn't that easy to switch off.

There was the slash at the corner of his mouth, for instance, that might once, when he was a little boy, have been a dimple. And a thick cowlick of honey-coloured hair was falling across his forehead in a way that demanded she reach across, slide her fingers through it, push it back.

She just wanted to touch him, she realised, and because this wasn't the time, or the place, she tucked her hands beneath her bottom and kept them out of harm's way…

But still her eyes ate him up, loving the way he looked so at ease with himself, comfortable…*lived in.*

'What?' he asked, when the waitress had poured them each a glass of wine and departed. 'What is it? Have I got a smudge of grease on my nose or something?'

Oh, Lord, she'd been caught staring. Shaking her head, she released her fingers to pick up her glass, take a sip of the dark red wine. Maybe he'd think the flush on her cheek was simply a reflection… 'Why did you split up from your wife?'

Well, he was the one who'd insisted on the getting-to-know-you break. Dan shrugged, scarcely knowing what to say about something that had happened so long ago. 'Maybe I wasn't the kind of husband she'd hoped for.'

'But she left her daughter…' She sat back quickly. 'I'm sorry. It's none of my business.'

'She wasn't particularly maternal, either.' *Just manipulative.* 'I should have anticipated that once the reality of sleepness nights and dirty nappies kicked in she would lose interest.'

'But didn't you say she'd just had a baby?'

'History repeating itself,' he said, without thinking, but Mandy didn't understand. Why should she? 'Vickie's latest lover is a lot older than she is.' *A lot older.* 'He's seriously rich, but childless. I've a feeling that she believes the production of an heir will ensure that the union becomes permanent. Don't worry, she won't repeat the mistake of abandonment a second time. And she has a nanny for all the tedious stuff.'

'Poor Sadie. How that must hurt.'

'Yes, I suppose it must.' No sympathy for him? Maybe she could tell he didn't need it. His only regret was that Sadie should be hurting. It was something he should have anticipated. 'But wasting her future isn't going to help her feel any better.'

'Maybe she doesn't care about feeling better. Maybe the point is to make her mother feel worse.'

'I doubt if she'd even notice.'

There were always ways of getting noticed, Amanda thought. Especially if you were bright, inventive, and hurting sufficiently not to care about the long-term consequences. 'What does she want to do?' Amanda asked as the waitress brought their food. 'Sadie?'

'What does any sixteen-year-old girl want? You tell me.'

Amanda picked up her fork, staring at the plate of mezze Daniel had ordered without really seeing it. She jabbed an olive, nibbled at it. When she had been sixteen she had been happy. She'd had a father who loved her, a mother who'd remembered enough about being sixteen to keep her from making stupid mistakes without being heavy-handed about it and an older brother she'd adored. That was what sixteen-year-old girls wanted, and there wasn't enough money in the world to buy that for Sadie. 'I'm sorry, Daniel, I don't think I can help you much with that one.' She looked up. 'Just keep loving her, no matter what she does.'

'Or how hard she makes it?'

'You've got the picture.' Then she grinned. 'Get her to twenty-three and she'll be past the worst.'

He groaned, more mock than serious. 'Right now that sounds like a life sentence.'

'With any luck it will be.'

'What?' Then, 'Oh, right—'

'Then you start all over again with the next generation.'

'You really know how to rub it in, Mandy Fleming.' But he, too, was grinning as he topped up her wine. 'I'm way too young to think about being a grandfather.'

'No man with a daughter of sixteen is too old to be thinking about it,' she pointed out.

'She's got more sense.'

Amanda speared a tiny grilled aubergine. 'This is good.'

'Hell, Mandy…' Amanda didn't answer, but her silence said more than words. 'She wouldn't.'

'No?'

'You're not really suggesting she would get pregnant deliberately?'

'I don't know her. But it would be horribly…fitting. If she were looking for some way to lash out. You think you're too young to be a grandfather,' she reminded him. 'Try and imagine how Sadie's mother would feel about becoming a grandmother.'

'Vickie would hate it.'

Amanda shrugged, point made.

Dan sat back in his seat, food apparently forgotten. 'No, I can't believe she'd do anything so stupid. Her life would be in ruins.'

'Hardly in ruins, but certainly messed up a bit, which would be a pity. You're sure she's spending her time working on a motorbike?'

'Yes. Yes, of course.' But Dan thought about it. He hadn't seen Bob. It could have been anyone in the car wash. 'At least…' Was it his imagination that Ned Gresham had been hanging around the garage a lot more than usual? Gresham wasn't the kind of man to waste time at the end of the day. He was on his feet even as the thought struck home. 'Will you excuse me while I make sure?'

Amanda picked up her glass, toasted her missing companion with a wry smile. 'Amanda, darling,' she murmured to herself, 'you certainly know how to ruin an evening.' Beth would probably say it was intentional. That she had cold feet. If she had, they were about the only part of her that was cold.

She waited as Dan slid back into the seat opposite her, a slightly sheepish grin across his face. 'She's just taken the motorbike for a test run.'

'Alone?'

'No, she's with Bob.'

She felt slightly silly. 'I'm sorry. I'm afraid I have a rather vivid imagination—'

'Don't apologise.' His hand covered hers on the table. 'You could have been right. For a minute there it sounded exactly the kind of thing she might do.' For a minute there, his blood had run quite cold. Now, looking at the lovely woman sitting too far away from him, he felt the kind of warmth that could, should, only have one outcome. He looked at her plate. She'd toyed with her food, eaten scarcely anything. 'Do you want that?' She shook her head, pushed the plate away. 'Come on, then. Let's go.'

'Go?'

He tossed some notes onto the table and, scooping her up by the arm, said, 'I've a pretty wild imagination myself, and right now it's working overtime.'

Amanda opened her mouth, closed it again. Then she said, 'Dating you is better than a diet.'

He hailed a passing cab. 'So, patent me.'

'You've got to be joking. I'm keeping you all to myself.' He opened the door for her, but didn't surrender her hand as he followed her aboard, gave the driver the address. 'You're seeing me to my door tonight, then?' she asked, her eyes glinting wickedly in the passing street lights.

'I try never to make the same mistake twice.'

They were there in two minutes. He paid off the driver and walked her to the door, took her key, unlocked it and waited. Amanda couldn't believe it. He was waiting for an invitation? Surely he realised…? Or maybe he wanted to give her one last chance… 'Would you like coffee?' she asked.

'I'll pass on the coffee, thanks.'

That didn't do it. 'A nightcap?' she offered.

'I'm driving.'

'Oh.' He was still waiting. Well, damn him, he could wait. 'I've got a video of *The English*—' He swept her through the door, backed her hard against the wall, holding her there with his body, his hands against the wall as he leaned into a kiss that came down on her mouth with the searing impact of a branding iron.

This was a world away from the sweetly delicate kisses which had sent them racing into the night to cool off. This was a world away from anything Amanda had ever experienced in her life before. There was nothing teasing or delicate about the way Daniel's mouth was burning hers, about the way his tongue was turning her mind to jelly, her legs to water.

Amanda's hands clutched at his shoulders, her fingers bunching the cloth of his jacket as she clung to him. She had no intention of letting him walk away a second time and, since her mouth was too busy to tell him so, she allowed her tongue to join his in a silken invitation that needed no words. Those big hands slid down the wall to cradle her, lift her against him. His heat licked against her thighs, permeated her clothes, and she was drowning in his scent, his taste. This, she decided, had nothing whatever to do with any baby plan. She wanted Daniel Redford for himself, and the knowledge wrought a soft moan of pleasure from her throat.

They had left the light on in the kitchen in their precipitate dash from the flat, and now, as he lifted his head, it spilled onto the face of man who was close to the edge.

'Say it!' he demanded. 'Say what you really mean…'

'We could watch it in bed,' she offered.

His only reply was the crash of the front door as he kicked it shut.

*   *   *

'Did I wake you?'

Amanda stretched beneath the soft white duvet. She felt blissfully, unbelievably happy, Daniel's scent filling her whole body, his voice in her ear. The only thing that would have been better would have been to have him there beside her to wake her with a kiss. She tucked the telephone more closely to her ear. 'Mmm. Thank you.'

'For the wake-up call?'

'For a whole lot of things, but that'll do to be going on with.' The floor was littered with her clothes, discarded in their race for the bed, without a thought for the morning. Without a thought for anything. Not that Daniel had been able to stay. She hoped Sadie hadn't been waiting up for him, or he'd have been in serious trouble—it must have been way past curfew when he'd finally got home. 'What are you doing?' she asked.

'Lying here, wishing I was with you. Trying to persuade myself to get up and go to work.'

'Get up and come over here instead. I'll keep you busy. And you never did have that coffee.'

'So much to do, so little time. Maybe tonight?'

She was desperately tempted, but she had been booked for months to give a talk at the secretarial college she had attended. 'I can't tonight. I'm working.'

'Not for Guy Dymoke, I hope?'

She laughed, basking in the warm glow of his possessiveness. 'You'd mind?'

'I'd insist on coming with you.'

'What a pity. I think I'd have enjoyed that. But I'm going to a function at my old secretarial college. Maybe tomorrow?'

'I think I'm going to have to devote the weekend

to Sadie—mend some fences, hopefully make her see sense. Monday?'

Monday seemed like a lifetime away. It was like being a teenager again. 'Monday will be fine, but don't expect me to cook—'

'Mandy…' She waited. 'We need to talk.'

He sounded so serious. She didn't want to be serious. 'You want phone sex?' she enquired.

He laughed right on cue. 'Thanks, but I'd rather wait for the real thing. Monday. I promise. One way or another.'

Amanda put the phone down, then swung her feet to the floor before the heady scent of Daniel could drag her back beneath the covers. She stripped the bed, stuffed the sheets in the washer, gathered her clothes, dumped them in her overnight bag and set about cleaning the apartment, obliterating every trace of her presence. Only then did she shower, put on the suit she had brought with her for the office. And it was still only eight o'clock.

'I take it you won't be begging me for a lift this morning?'

Sadie, dressed in bikers' leathers and with a terrifying black-visored helmet dangling by a strap from her arm, was on her way out by the time he made it to the kitchen.

'I wasn't sure you'd be up in time. It's no good setting curfews, you know, if you're not in to check up on me.'

'I trust you.'

'Big mistake.' Sadie's laugh was not pretty. 'You trusted my mother and just look where that got you.'

Dan, reminded uncomfortably of his moment of

panic in the wine bar, slotted some bread into the toaster, filled the kettle. 'I saw the bike,' he said. It had been parked up in the garage when he'd driven in last night. 'You'll make quite an impression when you ride into school on that next week.'

'Nice try, Dad, but I can't see the Warthog putting up with motorbikes at Dower House, can you? Not quite ladylike, darling,' she added, reverting to the aristocratic drawl. 'Such a pity I'm not old enough to drive a car. I have this hankering for a Mini Cooper, and somehow I think I could get just about anything I asked for right now, don't you?' The question was presumably rhetorical, since she didn't wait around for an answer, but headed for the front door. Halfway there she turned. 'It's my birthday in a couple of months, though.'

'Pass your re-sits and I might consider it.'

'Oh, well. I like the bike.'

'Wait until winter.' Then, 'I thought I might go down to the cottage for the weekend. It seems a pity not to make the most of this fine weather. Want to come?'

'Sure. Why not? If I don't come, you'll only take the earring queen and probably make a total fool of yourself.'

Almost certainly, he'd have said.

'Chasing young women will only get you into trouble, you know.'

'If that's a promise, forget the weekend. I'm making other plans.'

'Sorry, you invited me first, and since I'm not allowed to do anything more exciting, you're stuck with me.'

But Sadie's careless dismissal didn't fool him, he'd

seen the brightening in her eyes before she'd pulled on her crash helmet. The cottage had been a good idea.

'Now I really have to go. I have this absolute slave-driver of a boss, and if I'm even a minute late he threatens me with the Job Centre.' She waggled her fingers at him in a little wave. *'Ciao.'*

CHAPTER SEVEN

'OH, MY God,' Beth said from the doorway, when Amanda arrived at the office an hour later. 'That smile would give the Cheshire Cat an inferiority complex.'

Amanda hadn't been aware that she was smiling. She made an effort to look serious, but her face refused to co-operate and there wasn't a thing she could do about it. There wasn't a thing she *wanted* to do about it. 'Ask Jane to make some tea, will you?'

'Tea? You sit there looking like a cat who's had the sardines as well as the cream and you fob me off with demands for tea?'

'Earl Grey,' she elaborated. 'Then, if you could spare a few minutes, I've got the draft of the partnership agreement. We should go through it before we see the lawyers this afternoon.' She gave the document her total attention.

Beth ignored the hint that this was not something she wanted to talk about, along with the request for tea, and sat down opposite her. 'So?'

Well, no, she hadn't expected it to be that easy. 'So, what?'

'You look as if that chair is redundant. You appear to be floating.' Beth was smiling broadly, too. Perhaps it was infectious. 'I am seriously jealous. When's the baby due?'

'Aren't you rather jumping to conclusions?'

'You mean he took precautions?'

'I meant…' she began, then decided not to waste her breath. And of course Daniel had taken precautions. He was that kind of man. Thoughtful, caring—

'I should have anticipated that,' Beth said, interrupting the kind of thoughts that had no place in a well-run office. 'That's going to be a problem.'

'There's no rush.'

'That good, hmm? Well, better make hay while the sun shines, darling.'

Amanda glanced up. 'What's that supposed to mean?'

'Nothing. Except that you were planning a simple fun-filled fling, I seem to recall. It's always possible that he's on the same wavelength.'

'You're not that cynical, Beth.'

'I'm a realist, sweetie. And I've more experience with this lust-at-first-sight stuff than you have.'

Amanda made a determined effort to keep the smile in place. 'So, what would you suggest?'

'You could provide your own, er, precautions. Ready-doctored with a pin?'

Amanda gave up trying to get to grips with the legal jargon. 'And how would you feel if Mike decided he wanted a baby and did that to you?'

Beth paled. 'It's not the same.'

Amanda thought that it was exactly the same, but that two days ago, before she had fallen in love, she might very well have been tempted.

'Okay, forget the pin. But there must be a way.'

'No doubt. Now if we could just get on with some work?' Amanda waited, but Beth, apparently taking her partnership duties seriously, stayed where she was.

'Actually, there is a way.'

Amanda waited.

'You could tie him to the bed with your black silk stockings and drive him wild until he just can't help himself—'

'Silk stockings *and* whipped cream, Beth? I'm beginning to wonder about having you as a partner.'

'I'll make a great partner. I'm very imaginative.'

Amanda was trying very hard not to laugh. 'Then I suggest you apply your imagination to finding a secretary for Guy Dymoke. Someone whose shorthand won't desert her in the face of his killer smile.'

'I've already booked Jenna King,' Beth said. 'Amanda—'

'Tea?' she prompted.

'I just wondered if I have a home to call my own tonight. I only ask because if I'm staying at Mike's again I really need to get in a cleaning service—'

'Tonight I'm guest speaker at my old secretarial college, and Daniel is devoting the weekend to persuading his daughter to going back to school. We're hoping to get together on Monday, but I won't need your flat.'

'You're going to own up, then?'

'Of course.' Amanda wasn't exactly sure what she was going to say to Daniel, she only knew that she couldn't keep up the silly pretence that she was a temp. It was too important for that. He was too important for that. 'Well? Aren't you going to tell me that I'm making a big mistake? That he'll be stuffing the silverware in his jacket pocket—'

'No. You're right. Of course you must tell him.'

Amanda's cellphone rang before she could demand an explanation for this unexpected change of heart.

She picked it up and waited for Beth to leave, then pressed 'Receive'. On the point of answering with her usual 'Amanda Garland', a tingle at the base of her spine warned her to give the number instead.

'Mandy?' The tingle had been right and her heart skipped a beat at the sound of Daniel's voice. 'I know we agreed to see each other on Monday evening, but I was thinking, lunch today would be nice.'

Lunch would be wonderful. 'I thought you'd be working.'

'I am, but the boss lets me eat lunch. How's the old tartar on that subject?'

'That,' she replied, 'rather depends on what you mean by lunch.' There was a distant crash. 'Daniel? I do hope you're not driving?'

'No. No...'

'Good. So, lunch. What'll it be? Sandwiches by the Serpentine? Pizza in Pimlico? A roll—'

'Mandy—'

'—in Regent's Park?' she continued, without missing a beat.

'The Serpentine,' he said. 'I'll meet you at the Prince of Wales Gate at one o'clock.'

'Fine. I'll bring the sandwiches. Any requests?'

He just laughed, so she cut him off.

'Did you get into trouble last night?'

Daniel had been waiting for her at the gate when she'd arrived, a few minutes late. He hadn't said anything, had simply tucked her arm under one hand and taken the distinctive green and white carrier bag that held their lunch in the other and begun to walk with her towards the lake.

'Trouble?'

'For missing your curfew. Sadie didn't strike me as the kind of girl to miss an opportunity like that.'

'She isn't. She didn't. But with any luck she'll be back at school next week and then things will be easier.'

'You think she'll go?'

'Maybe.' He made for an empty bench and checked out the contents of the carrier. 'Sushi?'

'Don't you like it?'

'It's fine. Seaweed is very good for you.' The grin was even more lopsided than usual. 'So I've heard.'

'There are sandwiches.' She leaned forward. 'And I'm sure I asked for…yes, look, there's a Scotch egg.'

'Just one?'

She looked up and her mouth was inches from his. 'We could share it. You have the Scotch and I'll have the—'

His hand captured her head and his mouth momentarily stopped the words before he moved sharply back, almost as if he dared not trust himself. 'Oh, God, this is torture. I want to undress you and make love to you right here.'

'We'd frighten the ducks.'

'We'd get arrested. Can you take the afternoon off?' he asked, with a desperate urgency.

Amanda swallowed hard and forced herself to remember her appointment with the solicitor about the partnership at three, the decorator coming to look at the new offices at four-thirty. 'Not a chance.' Then, 'Can you?'

For one crazy moment he considered abandoning a meeting that could possibly bring him the biggest contract he was likely to get that year. Then he shook his head, but it was a close run thing. 'What about tomorrow?'

'I thought you were spending the weekend with Sadie?'

'Sadie will be slaving away with a tin of car wax until five o'clock,' he assured her. 'I want her to be feeling every muscle when I point out the advantages of returning to school.'

'I almost feel sorry for her.'

'Don't. She still owes you an apology.' He took her hand, turned it over, rubbed his thumb up the inside curve of her fingers. 'But just because she's working doesn't mean that I have to. We could spend the day together.'

'The whole day? You can really manage that?'

Amanda's face lit up at the prospect and Daniel knew that he should tell her the truth right then. What stopped him was the knowledge that she would instantly understand why he'd done it and be angry with him for not trusting her. Tomorrow, at the cottage, they would be alone, with all the time in the world for explanations, all the time in world to prove that he was sorry.

He helped himself to a cheese and pickle sandwich, tore off the corner and tossed it to a hopeful mallard, and said, 'No problem. I'll pick you up at the flat at ten, shall I?'

'Ten is fine. But the office would be better. I have some things to do there.'

'The Garland Agency?'

For a moment Amanda considered blurting it all out right there and then. But suppose he thought that she had been laughing at him? Making a fool of him?

He might change his mind about the day out. About her.

Tomorrow. She'd tell him tomorrow. If she picked her moment, she was almost sure he would see the funny side of it, and a little smile tugged at the corner of her mouth. 'Where will we go?'

'There's a weekend cottage that I use sometimes. It's very quiet.'

Amanda had been about to suggest asking her brother to loan them his place for the day. She was glad she hadn't.

'I won't be in the garage tomorrow, Sadie.'

She didn't bother to look up from the magazine she was flicking through. 'So? I don't need you to hold my hand.' She replaced the personal stereo headphones. 'No shortage of people willing to do that,' she added casually, as she reached for the switch.

Dan caught her wrist, keeping her attention—such as it was. 'So long as that's all they're holding.'

'What's the matter, Dad?' She finally raised her eyes, looked him full in the face. 'You can have fun with the earring queen, but I have to stay at home and revise maths, is that it?'

'You make choices, Sadie,' he said, 'and you live with the consequences. And that includes the consequences of holding hands with Ned Gresham.'

Beneath the white pancake make-up she was still young enough to blush. 'Ned's nice.'

'He's a good driver. "Nice" might be pushing it. "Nice" twenty-five year-old men aren't interested in schoolgirls.'

'I told you, I'm not going back to school.'

He refused to be sidetracked. 'He's too old, Sadie,

and I promise you, there are no shortage of full-grown women eager to catch his eye. Of course, there are considerable advantages to knocking up the boss's daughter.' He was being deliberately crude, hoping to strip away any romantic notions she might be harbouring. 'He wouldn't be the first man to come up with the idea.'

'Or the first woman. Isn't that how my mother does it?' Then she rubbed at one of the studs decorating her right ear. 'Just make sure it's not happening all over again.' She wasn't being exactly subtle. 'You had two cars when Mum used my imminent arrival to force your hand. Well, you were quite a catch in that neighbourhood, I should imagine. Of course, we slowed you down a bit—babies are expensive, expansion had to be put on hold for a while—so when something more exciting came along she didn't hesitate to jettison the baggage. Well, no need to beat about the bush. We both know that she's made something of a career out of it. She must be getting a bit desperate if she's had to revert to the original plan, though—'

'Sadie—'

'Actually, taking the long view, I suppose she did you a favour. I mean, you've come a long way since she walked out. But I have to tell you that Miss Mandy Fleming looks like a very expensive lady.'

'Not that expensive. She bought lunch.'

'Lunch?' Her eyes widened as she absorbed the implication of him seeing her again so soon. She shrugged, shook her head. 'Bad sign, Dad. She must be really serious.' Then the couldn't-care-less act crumbled and she peeled herself from the sofa and spun away from him as if she couldn't bear to look at him. 'Hell, she'll probably give you a baby, too, if that's what it takes to hook you. Or is that what you want? Has my little stepbrother given you ideas about a son of your own to follow in your footsteps? I don't suppose you'd make such a song and dance about it if he failed *his* bloody exams.' She headed for the door, turned there and looked back. 'Maybe I should try that one with Ned—'

'Sadie!'

'You know what they say. Like mother, like daughter…'

Dan was still trying to figure out what had just happened when her bedroom door slammed shut.

Amanda was speaking to the new intake at the secretarial college where she had honed her keyboard skills and learned to use a Dictaphone efficiently. She hadn't had time for shorthand. Her father hadn't had the time to wait.

She came along every year, hoping to inspire the girls to reach for stars. She had reached the point where she was encouraging them to come and see her after graduation when she felt a tingle at the base of her spine.

Daniel was thinking about her. She knew it, and for just a moment she lost her thread.

It was another half an hour before she could retreat to the principal's private loo, retrieve her mobile and call him.

'Daniel?'

'Mandy? I don't believe it. I was just wishing I could talk to you…'

'I know.'

'You knew?'

Even as she'd said the words she had realised how stupid they sounded. She'd just wanted him to be thinking about her. That was all… 'I mean, I was wishing the same. Is there a problem?'

'No. Not now. I just had a row with Sadie, that's all. Nothing new.'

'Do you want to take a raincheck on tomorrow?'

'Tomorrow, my darling, the sun is going to be shining and we are spending the day together. It's the one bright spark in what promises to be a very stormy weekend.'

'Ten o'clock, then.'

'I'll be counting the minutes.' *Counting the minutes.* A cliché. As clichéd as a troublesome teenager. But then that was what clichés were, he thought, and just because something was obvious that didn't mean that it was any less the truth.

For a while after her storming exit, the barrier of loud music had kept him from knocking on Sadie's door. She wouldn't have heard him anyway, or perhaps she was simply showing him that she wasn't in the mood to listen. Now, as he stowed his mobile back in its charger, he realised the music had stopped. If she'd lowered the drawbridge it was time to let her know that even if, for her mother, she had been little more than a device to get a wedding ring on her finger, he had loved her since the moment she'd erupted, bawling, into the world.

He tapped on the door. 'Sadie, can I come in?' There was no response, and when he tapped again the silence seemed to echo back at him. 'Sadie?' If she didn't want to talk this was the moment for the music to blast out once more. It didn't, and with a sudden sense of foreboding he turned the handle. The door wasn't locked. But then she wasn't there. Her bedroom and bathroom were empty; the only sign of life was the light on the music system. The CD she had put on to cover her escape had finally come to an end, but it had done its job.

'Trousers in the office? What kind of message is that giving the world, Miss Garland? Image is everything!' Beth was taking her new partnership terribly seriously.

Amanda, bending over the drawing of the ground-floor office plan, didn't bother to look up. 'You sound exactly like my old headmistress.'

'Do I? How was she?'

'Sorry?'

'Your old headmistress. Last night.'

'Oh, not at the secretarial college. At Dower House. There's a letter from her this morning, asking me if I'll give the inspirational speech at prize-giving next term.'

'Your fame is spreading.'

'No, the star former pupil who was first choice was promoted in the latest Government reshuffle and she's had to pull out because of pressure of work. I'm just next on the list.'

'Well, it's great anyway.'

'Is it? Last night was in the nature of a recruiting drive. I don't imagine too many of the Dower House girls will be interested in temping and I can't believe that she's going to want to hold up a single mother as an example to her "gels".'

'You might not get pregnant for months, and just think of all those wealthy fathers and mothers who'll be in the audience. Exactly the kind of people who'll be needing secretaries, nannies, whatever. It'll be great for business.'

'I'm not sure that Pamela Warburton would appreciate that sentiment.'

'No? So why does she invite ex-pupils who are Members of Parliament or successful businesswomen to her speech days, if it's not to make a good impression, drum up new business?' She had the self-satisfied smile of a woman who knows she's right. 'Ring her now and say yes.'

'And if I'm like a ship in full sail?'

'You'll be living proof that a woman can have everything she wants without a man to hold her hand. What better example is there than that? Is that the ground-floor plan?'

'Mmm. What do you think?'

'I think you should put it away, forget about work for today and enjoy yourself.' Beth gathered up the plan.

'Hey! I was looking at that.'

'You'll have the whole weekend to look at plans. Sit down and have a cup of coffee to calm your nerves. Where are you going?'

'Some cottage Dan's borrowed. It can't be far; he's got to be back in London by six to pick up his daughter.'

'Borrowed?'

'Well, yes.' She took her first sip of coffee in days. It tasted wonderful. You could have too much herb tea, she decided. 'What's wrong with that?'

'Did I say anything was wrong?'

'No. It was all in the tone of your voice. Is there something I should know?'

Beth took refuge behind her coffee cup.

'Come on,' Amanda persisted. 'What aren't you telling me?'

'Nothing. You didn't want to know.'

'About Daniel? But that was before…' She stopped on the brink of giving herself away.

'Before you fell hook, line and sinker?' Beth shook her head. 'You weren't listening to me, sweetheart. *He* was the one who was supposed to be hooked. Coarse fishermen release their quarry once it's served its purpose.' Amanda's brows rose. 'Once it's been weighed and won the prize.'

Amanda refused to be sidetracked. 'What have you done?'

'Nothing!' Then, just a touch defensively, 'Someone has to look after your best interests. I got a friend to do a little checking, that's all.'

'Oh, Beth. I told you not to. That is just so tacky…' Beth simply raised her eyebrows. 'All right. What is it? If it's something bad I'd rather know now.'

'Did I say it was bad? The man is squeaky clean, I promise. Triple A credit rating, pays his taxes, helps old ladies across the road…'

'But?'

'But that doesn't mean he isn't keeping secrets.'

'What secrets?' Her pulse-rate picked up as if she had been taking vigorous exercise.

Beth extracted a large manila envelope from her bag, but then, infuriatingly, she hung onto it. 'You don't want this. I'm sure he'll tell you himself today.'

'Tell me what?'

'It's nothing important. Really.'

'I swear—'

The intercom buzzed from Reception. 'Miss

Garland, there's someone asking for Miss Mandy Fleming. You wanted to know.'

'I'll be right there.' She caught Beth's eye. 'All right. So, I keep secrets too.'

'Exactly.'

'I'm going to tell him today.'

'Then I've every confidence that he'll do the same. You're right. This is tacky and I'll put it in the shredder right now…'

But Amanda blocked the way, holding out her hand for the envelope in a manner that brooked no resistance.

'Just promise me you won't read it until you get home,' Beth insisted. 'Give him a chance to tell you himself.' Amanda was promising nothing. 'Curiosity killed the cat, remember.'

'Just hope, when I've read this, that I don't kill you.'

Daniel was leaning against the Jaguar when Mandy appeared behind the glass door of the Garland Agency, too busy tucking something into the side pocket of her big shoulder bag to notice him. Then she looked up and saw him and smiled and he was blown away. She was so lovely. And for today she was all his.

He crossed the pavement to meet her as she opened the door, took her hand, kissed her cheek, breathed in the delicious floral scent of her skin that only a lover would ever be close enough to fully appreciate. She looked up at him and for just a moment he thought that she looked tense, a little uncertain. Then she grinned. 'Does the boss know you've borrowed the Jaguar?'

'He lets me have it whenever I want.'

'Really? Why?'

'It's a long story.'

She glanced up at him. 'One you're going to tell me?'

There was a directness in that look that left no hiding place, and something warned him that time was running out on playing games. 'Yes, Mandy. It's one I'm going to tell you,' he said. He opened the passenger door and she slid onto the big worn leather seat that seemed to swallow her up, then she reached out and ran her fingers along the rich walnut veneer of the dash. 'It's irresistible, isn't it?' he said, sliding in beside her. 'Would you like to drive her?'

'Now?' Her eyes lit up. 'You're kidding me? She must be your pride and joy.' He'd meant in the quiet lanes around the cottage, but perhaps it was time to give her his trust, one hundred per cent. She'd already got everything else. But when he offered her the keys she shook her head and laughed. 'That's brave of you, Daniel, but I'll pass for the moment. I'm used to driving something a lot smaller in London.'

'Are you? What do you drive?'

Amanda thought about her precious little MG, presently residing in the mews garage, smaller in size, but a lot more powerful than the Jaguar. And she wished she'd kept her mouth shut.

'Something small and green from British Leyland,' she said. It had been having a major service the day of the seminar at The Beeches or she'd never have met Daniel.

'Very wise. This beauty drinks petrol like a thirsty camel, and getting spares is a nightmare. I don't take her out every day.' He glanced at her. 'But this is a special occasion.'

'I thought you were looking pleased with yourself. Has Sadie relented?'

He'd been referring to spending the day with her. But perhaps he was getting a bit carried away. 'Not quite,' he said, fitting the key into the ignition. 'But I have high hopes. She has seriously blotted her copy-book and she knows it.'

CHAPTER EIGHT

IT WAS every parent's worst nightmare. A troubled teenager running out into the night. Or rather riding out into the night, because of course she'd taken the bike.

For a moment he had held onto the faint hope that she might have gone next door to Annabel. A phone call had soon put paid to that idea, and, cursing himself for every kind of idiot for indulging her, he'd phoned Bob, phoned the few friends she had in London who weren't away at school, praying that she'd been simply trying to create a drama, scare him.

In that, she had succeeded, but panicking wouldn't help. He'd even, as a last resort, phoned Vickie's mother and suffered an earful of abuse for his pains, but once he'd realised that Sadie wasn't with her grandmother he'd cut the woman short; he hadn't had time for her 'sins of the flesh' lecture.

After that there had been nothing left to do but cruise the streets, hoping to see the bike parked outside some burger bar with Sadie inside, comforting her misery with junk food. He'd found it, finally, outside the café opposite the garage, but his relief had been short-lived. The lights had still been on, but it had just closed.

That had left only one place she could be. The office didn't open at night, but there were always lights on in the yard; getting people to where they needed to be was, after all, a twenty-four hours a day, seven days a week business. He'd nodded to the security guard and walked in.

Ned Gresham had had a late afternoon pick-up from a liner docking at Southampton, and Dan hadn't doubted that Sadie knew that as well as he did. He'd come back; the Lexus booked for the job in its bay, the yard quiet, only the security lights on. Then, as he'd turned away, the interior light had come on as the driver's door clicked open and he'd heard Gresham say, 'Don't be silly, Sadie. Go home. Your dad'll be wondering where you are.'

'I'm not a kid! I'm sixteen, you know. Look, I'll prove it to you…' She'd unzipped her leathers.

Even across the width of the yard Dan had been able to see that she'd had nothing on beneath them, but his surge forward had been abruptly halted by Gresham's bored, 'Yeah, yeah, very nice, Sadie. But if you want to get laid pick on someone your own age.'

'You—' Sadie had given the man a virtuoso demonstration of her grasp of Anglo Saxon.

'Sure, kid. Whatever you say. Now beat it. I've got a date.'

Amanda gasped as he related the story. 'The poor child. She must have been absolutely mortified. What on earth did you do?'

'Beat a strategic retreat before either of them saw me. I was sitting watching the late news when she crept in ten minutes after me—the longest ten minutes in my entire life, let me tell you—and when she left for the garage this morning, she was what I can only describe as subdued.'

'She went into work this morning? Oh, my.'

'I know. I actually went so far as to say I didn't

think she looked too good, that maybe she should stay at home—despite the fact that would have meant cancelling today.'

'I'd have understood, Daniel. Sadie has to come first.'

'Yes, well...she said she was fine, and that Bob was counting on her. She even offered to do the shopping for the weekend.' He glanced across at her. 'Despite everything I'm going to really miss her when she goes back to school next week.'

'Well, you'll see her in the evenings.'

He frowned. 'No.' Then, 'I'm sorry, I thought you realised. She's at boarding school. At Dower House. But I think once she's done those re-sits I'll suggest we call it a day. She can switch to a sixth form college in London for her A levels next year.'

'She's at Dower House?'

'What's the matter? Don't you approve of boarding schools? It was her decision—'

Amanda shook her head. 'No. I told you. I went to boarding school.' And for a working man, on his own, it made sense. If he could afford it. 'It's just that I went to Dower House.'

'Did you? Small world.'

'Yes. Isn't it?'

They'd reached the motorway and Daniel put his foot down so that the huge old car leapt forward, eating up the road. Scarcely the moment for a heart to heart.

Instead she found a tape and slotted it into the cassette, glancing out of the window at the aircraft lifting off as they sped passed Heathrow, trying to get to grips with the fact that Daniel's daughter went to one of the most expensive schools in the country.

She hadn't told him that she owned her Knightsbridge home, drove a sports car and ran her own highly successful business despite the fact that she had the kind of private income that made working for a living a choice rather than a necessity. And all because she hadn't wanted to make him feel uncomfortable. At least she hoped that was why she'd kept quiet.

But he had money. That was his secret. That was what Beth had hinted at. She had checked him out and she knew.

So what had Daniel done? Won the football pools? Or the lottery? Could he be one of those eccentrics who, when they won a fortune, vowed it wasn't going to change their life? Just provided his daughter with the best education that money could buy. Indulged his love of old and beautiful cars.

Beth's envelope was practically burning a hole in the side of her bag. Amanda touched it, her fingers easing along the open end; the report was right there. For a wild moment she even considered taking it out, reading it while he was concentrating on the road, but even as her fingers tightened around it he took the same slip-road as he had a week earlier. Took the same road up through the beech woods.

He glanced at her with a smile that never failed to make her knees goes weak. 'It's not far now.'

She let the envelope go, let her hands lie in her lap, fingers entwined, and five minutes later he stopped outside an old forestry cottage that lay in an isolated clearing in the woods. The dull green paint had been stripped away from ornate bargeboards trimming the steeply pointed gables and were now, like the windows and doors, coated in fresh white gloss. It looked well cared for and welcoming, surrounded by a small garden filled with late summer flowers.

'This is it.'

He was watching her, suddenly tense. 'It's charming,' she said. 'Hansel and Gretel without the candy.'

He relaxed, laughed. 'Yeah, well, I'm the wicked witch and I'm going to eat you all up.' He looped his arm about her waist and lifted her across the gearstick and into his lap. Then he kissed her, long and hard and sweet, and by the time she'd come up for air he was busy making good his promise, taking his mouth on a forage over her chin and down her throat, disposing of buttons with dizzying efficiency. By the time he'd unhooked her bra and his breath was a teasing warmth against her breasts she'd long since consigned Beth and her envelope to the devil.

Then she began to giggle. 'What?' He had lifted his head, and any desire to laugh instantly evaporated in the heat haze of his eyes.

'We're making love in a car like a couple of teenagers,' she protested, then swallowed as the corner of his mouth slowly lifted to smile right back at her.

'When I was a teenager I didn't have a car.' The smile faded, but the intensity remained. 'Not that it was a problem…' And he released the door catch and he went with it, taking her down with him onto the grass. It was thick and soft and crackly with the dry leaves that had drifted from the huge old beech trees. 'How's that?' he asked.

How was that? His arm about her waist, holding her against his chest, hip to hip, their legs entangled, the warm touch of his cheek against her face? It was everything she had ever dreamed of. And the remainder of his shirt buttons surrendered as she proceeded to demonstrate just how good it was.

For a moment he was tempted to just lie back and let it happen. But fifty yards away there was a bed… 'Mandy, behave yourself,' he said, laughing, as she tugged the cloth free.

'Not a chance.'

Well, he hadn't really meant it, Dan decided as the cool autumn air raised gooseflesh on his chest. But not for long, and then, like the buttons, he gave up any pretence at fighting the desire that ripped through him.

Everything about her was spare, elegant. Her breasts were taut and incredibly beautiful, he thought as she lifted herself so that he could shuck down her trousers, cradle that sweet backside in his hands. She was silk and lace and linen sheets and four-poster beds, a lifetime away from a teenage tumble in the long grass. Maybe that was why the long grass was, in the end, irresistible.

Amanda had lost it. The ice maiden, the virgin queen—all those names assigned to hurt when she was in the sixth form—had finally lost it. Not the minor technical detail of her virginity; she'd disposed of that with the efficiency she applied to everything she set her mind to. But in her head and in her heart, where it really mattered.

Oh, she'd had a couple of relationships that should have been right, relationships with men who, in the eyes of her family, her friends, had seemed perfect. But they hadn't been, and now she knew why. There had been no magic.

Now she was lying practically naked in some

woodland glade in the arms of Daniel Redford and suddenly the world was lit up with fairy dust.

She should be ashamed of herself for behaving like some lost-in-love teenager, but she wasn't. She was some lost-in-love woman, and, having dealt with the belt of Daniel's trousers, she turned her attention to getting him out of them.

'Mandy?' Her lips trailed across his, putting a stop to speech, demanding his immediate attention, and he willingly obliged. And later, when he recalled what he had been about to say, he didn't bother. For some reason it didn't seem in the least bit important. Instead he said, 'We're really going to have to make it to a bed before we do that again.'

'Can't take it, huh?'

'That, and the fact that I'm lying on a conker.'

She looked up and then grinned. 'You can't be. Those are beech trees.'

'I promise you, from where I'm lying it feels like a conker.' He caught her round the waist and sat up. 'What shall we do now?'

'Get dressed?'

'Why waste time?'

'We could go for a walk,' she suggested.

'The furthest I'm walking is to the front door.'

'It's a bit early for lunch,' she said, retrieving her shirt and pulling it on. 'But I suppose we could do something to work up an appetite.'

He grinned. 'I'll show you round first.'

'I knew it. You're just playing for time.'

He stood up, pulled her to her feet. 'You were the one who pointed out that I could become a grandfather any day.'

'You'll be glad to hear that it's not compulsory.'

'Only because Ned Gresham is a better man than I gave him credit for.' He picked up her bag from where it had tumbled out of the car and handed it to her. In fact, he thought, Ned Gresham had considerably more self-control than he'd just exhibited.

Daniel let them in through the back door of the cottage. It wasn't big, but he showed her everything. The neat little kitchen, the scullery, the pantry, the woodstore. The living room was furnished for comfort rather than style, with thick curtains and carpets to keep out the winter draughts and an enormous sofa stretched out in front of an big open fireplace. Amanda loved it. It felt right, and smelled of wood and lavender and history.

Upstairs there were a couple of bedrooms and a newly installed bathroom.

He showed her them all without comment, although she was aware that he was watching her closely. The tour concluded in the main bedroom. It was simply furnished with plain, neutral weaves and furniture that had been made from timber cut from the woods surrounding the cottage. Amanda crossed to the small-paned window, somehow feeling that her reaction mattered to Daniel, but not sure why. 'There's a field behind those trees,' she said, rather stupidly.

'Yes. It's where I taught Sadie to ride a motorbike. And drive a car. In fact a car is the next item on her shopping list.' He joined her at the window, looking at her rather than the view. 'I didn't borrow the cottage, Mandy. It's mine.'

'Yours?' Well, yes. That made sense. But why pretend? Why—?

'Oh, hell. Look, I was going to tell you later, but this is so stupid. I'm not a chauffeur, Mandy. I own

Capitol Cars. I built it up from scratch and now—well, it's pretty successful.'

And suddenly everything fell into place. It was so obvious when you knew. Daniel Redford wasn't a man to sit on his backside twiddling this thumbs and waiting for his numbers to come up on a Saturday night. He'd worked for everything he had. *So why hadn't he told her?* She'd had the excuse that she was sparing his feelings, men had such tender little egos…

'I started with one car twenty years ago.'

'I see.' She didn't. It didn't make sense.

'You're not angry?'

'Angry?'

'I should have told you, but…'

'Why on earth would I be angry?'

For a moment he thought he'd got away with it. That it was going to be all right.

Amanda wasn't angry. She was absolutely livid. He had played the humble chauffeur and she'd fallen for it. What on earth had Beth been thinking of, not telling her? And what the hell had he been thinking of? Did he know who she was after all? Was this his idea of a joke? Well, it wouldn't do to have him think she had no sense of humour, would it? So she laughed. 'Very good, Daniel.' She laughed again. Hell, she was going to laugh until she cried. The tears were already there, stinging the backs of her eyes.

'Mandy…' He said her name uncertainly, and then she knew it wasn't funny at all. Not a joke.

'I'm sorry. I should have told you.'

No. Not a joke. Quite deliberate. 'Why didn't you?' He didn't answer and his silence damned him. 'Oh, I see.' Well, of course she saw. It was as plain as the nose on his face. After all, hadn't she done exactly the same thing? Oh, she'd dressed it up, told herself that she was protecting him, that she hadn't wanted him to feel awkward. But hadn't there been, at the back of her mind, that insidious, nasty little suspicion planted by Beth that if he knew what she was, knew all that she had, he might just think he'd fallen on his feet? And with self-condemnation the anger seeped away from her as quickly as it had come. She was sorry, too. Sorry that neither of them had been brave enough to take a risk.

'I should have told you,' he repeated. 'I was going to when you came to the garage. I was going to invite you into my office and show you exactly what you'd turned down.'

At least he'd cared enough to be angry. 'And I ruined it all by arriving early and finding you beneath a car in your overalls like…' Like the man she'd thought he was. The man she had fallen in love with.

'I was going to tell you when I saw you that night, but—'

'But I jumped you before you could,' she said.

'Was I complaining?' Miserably she shook her head. 'Hey, come on. It's not that bad. It could have been worse.' It was. She still had to tell him that she'd been lying, too. 'I could have told you I was a millionaire and really been a pauper.'

'Are you? A millionaire?'

He shrugged. 'I suppose so. On paper, anyway. Most of it's tied up in the business, or in property.'

'It still counts.'

'Does it? I've never really thought about it. I really haven't been thinking very straight this past week, if you want to know the truth.'

'Yes, Daniel, I'd like to know the truth. And when you've told me your truth, I'll tell you mine…'

He lifted his hand, picked a leaf from her hair, brushed it back from her face. She couldn't bear to look up, see what was in his eyes. Instead she let her head fall against his chest. She wouldn't look until she'd told him everything. But his hand was cradling her cheek, the warmth of his fingers seeping into her soul. He kissed her temple, her cheek…

'Look at me, Mandy.'

And she looked, because it was quite beyond her to resist him.

'The truth, my darling girl, is that I love you—'

'Well, isn't that a pretty scene?'

Sadie was standing in the doorway. Black hair, black leathers, face dead white, but not with make-up. And in her hand was a brown manila envelope, the white typewritten pages of a report.

'Sadie?' Daniel sounded confused, not quite able to comprehend the arrival of his daughter. 'I thought you were at the garage.'

'I was. But then I thought I'd come down to the cottage early. I told Bob and he said it was a great idea. I was going to light the fire, prepare something special for dinner. For you. Because you've been great this week. Really. I wanted to repay you for that. I didn't think I'd have to share our special place with *her*.'

'Sadie—' Amanda made a move to forestall what she knew was coming.

'Don't you call me Sadie. Only my friends can call me Sadie and you are nothing but a tart on the make. Just like my mother.' Her blue eyes flashed. 'I wanted to repay you, Dad. Well, this should do it.' She lifted the typescript she was holding and held it out to him. 'Did your ''darling girl'' tell you that she'd hired a private investigator to check up on you?' At her back, Amanda felt Daniel go very still. 'Family background, marital status, credit rating, business... Everything you own. It's all there. The garage, the riverside penthouse, this place—all detailed down to the last brick, the last wheel nut.'

'Where did you get that?' Daniel didn't sound much different. His voice was still thick with emotion. Wrong emotion. 'Have you been looking through Mandy's bag?'

'There was no need. I didn't need to snoop. I found it outside. On the grass. By the car. It must have fallen out when you were...'

'Sadie, go downstairs. Now.'

She shrugged. 'Sure. I'll put the kettle on, shall I? I'm sure Miss Fleming would like a cup of tea before she leaves.'

Sadie's rubber-soled boots made scarcely a sound as she retreated to the ground floor, but her footsteps seemed deafening in the silence that closed about them in the bedroom.

'Mandy...'

'Don't.' Amanda took a step away from him. After that it was easier. 'Please, don't.'

'Is it true?'

No. And yes. And which would he believe? Which, given the evidence, would she believe? She saw from the way he'd stopped looking at her, stopped quite meeting her gaze, that he had already decided.

'When Vickie decided that she wanted me to marry her she got herself pregnant—'

'All by herself—'

'She stopped using a contraceptive and when she was carrying Sadie she told me that she would have an abortion if I didn't marry her.' He turned to the window. 'Just now. Out there…'

She knew what he was going to say. It was the age of responsible sex and just now, out there in the long, sweet grass, they'd behaved like a couple of careless teenagers on a lustful high. It had been crazy, and stupid, and that was bad enough. She wouldn't let him defile what had happened with anything worse. 'Please, don't worry. Marriage is the furthest thing from my mind. You have my promise that whatever happens you'll never see or hear from me again.'

Well? Wasn't that the way it was supposed to be? Hadn't that been the plan? She was trying, belatedly, to tuck her shirt into her trousers, but her fingers refused to co-operate. Well, they kept hoping that he'd say something. Tell her not to be silly. That they needed to talk. Offer to take her home. Instead he just stood there, looking at her as if she were a stranger.

Well, that was all part of the plan, too. But she had to get out of there before those tears that had earlier threatened became fact, and, giving up the shirt as a bad job, she turned and stumbled down the stairs.

Sadie was waiting for her in the living room, arms folded, a look of triumph on her face. It was sufficiently chilling to stop the shakes, and Amanda picked up her bag, retrieved her cellphone and asked directory enquiries to connect her to a local taxi service. Then, as the final humiliation, she was forced to ask Sadie where she was. The name of the road. The nearest junction.

'You can wait for it outside,' Sadie said, when it was done. And Amanda heard the tiny betraying shake behind all that black leather and bravado. Well, if she'd been Sadie, wouldn't she be bitter too? And afraid. Her mother had clearly never wanted her—not *her*, not a baby of her own to love. She had been simply a weapon to catch a man who had been on the up, easy to abandon when something better came along. And now some woman was trying to steal her father away from her, too.

The child had come too close to disaster already; right now she needed the undivided love of the one parent she could rely on. Well, that was fine. She hadn't been planning a future with Daniel, had she? Just a little romantic interlude. No strings attached.

But in the doorway she turned back. 'Go back to school, Sadie. You owe him that.'

'So that you can get your claws back into him the moment I've gone? Do you think I'm crazy? I'm staying put.'

Not crazy. Afraid. 'Just until you've taken your exams,' she urged. 'He'll let you go to sixth form college in London afterwards.'

'Oh, sure.'

'Ask him. He wants you home.' A shadow of uncertainty crossed the girl's pale face. 'Get real, Sadie. I'm no threat. Do you honestly think he'll want to see me again?'

But Sadie wasn't falling for that. 'Swear you'll stay away from him,' she demanded. And maybe she was right to, because it was a lot harder than Amanda could ever have imagined to say those words. Somewhere, deep down in her psyche, lurked a fantasy that eventually Daniel would discover the truth. Come after her. That it would be all right. 'Swear it!' Sadie persisted.

'If I do, you'll go back to school?' Sadie glared, then finally she nodded. 'Then I swear it.' And with those few words she did them both a favour and consigned her fantasy, along with the magic and the fairy dust, to the world of make-believe where they belonged.

The only thing that made it bearable, the only thing that kept her going as she walked down to the main road to meet her taxi, that stopped her from crumpling into a heap on the lane and sobbing her heart out, was the knowledge that he had loved her. He had said so, and for one moment it had undoubtedly been true.

That he would never believe her even if she told him until the end of time that she returned his love a hundred, a thousandfold, was nobody's fault but her own.

CHAPTER NINE

'IT'S today, isn't it? Your appointment at the clinic.' Amanda had been vaguely conscious of Beth hovering about her like an anxious mother hen all morning. 'Would you like me to come with you?'

'No need,' she said briskly. It hadn't occurred to her that Beth would remember the actual date of the clinic appointment, but then, knowing Beth, she'd probably written it in her own diary as a reminder to keep the day clear so that she could come along and hold her hand. She was that kind of friend.

'Is Jilly coming with you? Or your mother? I don't think you should go on your own.'

She'd hoped to keep her secret for a few weeks longer, but it seemed that she'd just run out of time. 'I'm not going.'

'What?' Beth moved away from the door, took the seat in front of her desk. 'You mean you've changed your mind about having a baby?'

'No. I simply mean that I am not going to the clinic. I cancelled the appointment a couple of weeks ago.'

'But why?' Beth didn't wait for an answer. She clearly thought she knew why. 'Look, darling, I don't know what happened between you and Daniel but you have to put it behind you. He was nothing but a diversion, remember? You're back on the main road now. You have to move on. A biological clock waits for no man,' she prompted. Then, 'And what about all those vitamins? The folic acid? The spinach.'

'What about them?'

'Well...' For a moment Beth floundered. 'It would be a pity to waste them.'

'Nothing is ever wasted. All experience is valuable—' Even as she spoke Amanda experienced the need to cut short their conversation, race to the cloakroom and throw up. When she finally emerged from the cubicle Beth was waiting for her, arms folded, leaning back against the vanity unit.

'That stuff you were saying about all experience being valuable,' she said, as Amanda splashed cold water onto her face. 'In what category would you place morning sickness?' She was grinning.

Well, Amanda had known she would find it amusing; she should probably just be grateful that Beth wasn't actually rolling on the floor laughing. In her place, she'd probably think it was funny, too.

Amanda regarded her reflection without pleasure. For the first time in her life she did not look anything like a model for the professional woman. She looked pasty, and there were dark rings around her eyes. Nothing to do with the fact that she was pregnant, but it explained why Beth's usually infallible antennae had missed the more obvious signs of early pregnancy. Even the nausea.

'So much for your faith in vitamin B6. I thought it was supposed to prevent morning sickness?'

'That's the theory. But only if you take it for a whole month before...er...' Beth's eyes were sparkling with mischief. 'Well, *you know*.'

'It isn't funny, Beth. It was a mistake.'

'In what way a mistake? I thought this was exactly what you planned?'

Never in a year of Sundays would she have planned this. 'It was a mistake to allow myself to be diverted…'

'Oh, I see.' Then she shrugged. 'So, if it's a girl you can call her Serendipity.' Amanda stared at her blankly. 'A happy accident.' Then, less certainly, 'You are happy about it? The baby? I mean, it was what you wanted?'

How could she be other than happy? She wanted a baby, and to be granted the gift of a child by the man she loved was more, far more, than she deserved. 'I didn't mean having a baby…I meant Daniel.' But then she'd always known that taking a diversion was taking a risk, stepping into the unknown. She'd gone to find him at the garage knowing that. She should have told him the truth then. Or later, at the wine bar. She'd had her chance then and hadn't taken it. But neither had he.

'Well, at least you don't have to agonise about whether you should tell the father.' That was Beth. She could always put an optimistic spin on the worst situation. It was probably what kept her falling in love even when experience suggested that loving and hurting were two sides of the same coin.

'No,' she agreed. 'No agonies there.' So why did it hurt so much? Because she knew, deep down, that despite everything he had said, despite the fact that she had told him that he would never hear from her again, she knew Daniel would want to know about this baby? It was that other promise, the one wrung from her as she'd left the cottage, that would keep her secret safe from him. Because she was very afraid that this baby, her father's baby, might prove the last straw for Sadie. And so far Sadie was back on course.

She'd phoned Pamela Warburton on the pretext of turning down her invitation to speak at the school prize-giving and she'd asked about the girl.

'Mercedes Redford? Do you know the family?'

'Not well.' At least not in the sense that Pamela Warburton meant 'know'. 'But I met, er, Mercedes—"*Mercedes?*"—and I wondered if she'd decided to come back and do her re-sits.'

'Yes, thank goodness. I really had no alternative but to suspend her for a week, but afterwards I wondered if she'd rather pushed me into it. Attention-seeking, you know. Well, there are family problems.'

'Yes, I know.'

'She's just staying until she's retaken her exams, then she's going to work with her father until she starts at her sixth form college next September. It's obvious that she can't wait to leave.'

'Maybe she'll be happier at home. You won't mention that I was asking about her, will you? I wouldn't like her to think I was checking up on her.'

'But you are.'

Yes, she had been. Well, her pregnancy test had just proved positive and perhaps, beneath all that care and consideration, she'd simply been hoping that Sadie had broken her word, thus releasing her from her promise.

'Now, are you sure I can't persuade you to do speech day for me?' Just the gentlest hint of blackmail had hung in the air.

'Pamela, I'd love to do it, but I think you should know that I'm pregnant. By speech day I won't be able to stand close enough to the rostrum to read my notes.'

'Then speak without them.'

'Do you really want an expectant single mother giving a bunch of impressionable girls the you-can-have-it-all speech?'

'You would appear to be the perfect example of that ideal, Amanda. I'll send you a letter confirming the date and time…'

Yes, well, it was an ideal she'd thought she had achieved too. How wrong could you be?

'Maybe whatever happened was for the best,' Beth said now, her anxious voice dragging her back from the slippery slope her thoughts were headed down.

The best. 'Of course it was. Everything has worked out exactly as planned.' *Exactly as planned.* She had nothing to complain about and she wouldn't. Her business was expanding; she was expecting the baby she had longed for. And from somewhere she found a smile with which to reassure Beth, because Beth, if she knew what had happened, would blame herself, and it wasn't her fault. It wasn't anyone's fault.

Amanda had refused to speak about the break-up. Merely said that it was over, that it wasn't a subject for conversation.

She and Daniel had both been playing the same stupid game, protecting themselves from the possibility of hurt, but Beth hadn't seen that, she had just seen the comic side of it and had assumed that when the facts came out they would, all three of them, have a good laugh about it. Beth, she suspected, had been playing matchmaker in earnest. And it had so nearly worked.

* * *

It was the middle of January before Daniel saw her again. At the theatre. Inevitably. A first night. Sadie's Christmas present for him. Perhaps she'd noticed that he wasn't getting out much and had thought he would be roused to find some nice, unpredatory woman to take with him. Not even for Sadie had he been able to manage that, and so his theatre-hating daughter had decided she'd have to go with him, just to make sure he took his medicine. She'd even bought a dress for the occasion.

It was black, of course. Well, one step at a time. Black and far too sexy for a girl who'd just turned seventeen, but with her height and her dramatically cropped hair there was no doubt that she was a head-turner. As heads turned to follow her progress across the foyer he suspected she might, after all, be enjoying herself.

He suspected she was wishing Ned Gresham was there to see her and see what he was missing. But Ned had found himself another job. The man was a good driver, and Dan had been sorry to lose him, but not sorry enough to ask him to reconsider leaving. He had the feeling that Ned felt about his daughter the way he felt about Mandy. They were both safer at a distance.

'I'll get a programme; you get the drinks,' Sadie said as they checked their coats.

He fought his way to the bar, bought a couple of tonic waters. Sadie wouldn't want to be seen with cola, and he… Well, he knew from experience how easy it would be to fall into a bottomless glass. He'd done it once when Vickie had presented him with her *fait accompli*. He'd come close a second time when she'd walked out on him. Both times because his life had been messed up and there hadn't been a damn thing he could do about it.

This time it was different. This time he could do something about it, and he knew that if he succumbed to liquid temptation, when he crawled out of the bottom of the whisky bottle he'd find himself hammering on the door of the Garland Agency demanding, begging, that someone tell him where he could find Mandy Fleming. He knew because even without the whisky, he'd been hard put to it to stop himself.

If only he hadn't found out. Ignorance was bliss, and he couldn't shake the nagging feeling that he would have been blissfully happy if he'd never found out what she'd been up to. Why on earth had she had the damned report with her? Why on earth had she been careless enough to drop it where Sadie could find it? Why on earth had Sadie chosen that day, of all days, to play the perfect daughter?

'Hey, I've seen this woman on television,' Sadie said, flipping through the programme. 'And him.' She looked pleased. As if it wasn't going to be quite the ordeal she had anticipated.

Poor Sadie. She'd worked so hard to find out what he would have chosen to see, if he'd been in the mood for entertainment. It had only been when it was too late, when he'd opened the envelope she had put on the Christmas tree for him, that he'd realised the reason for her sudden interest in the arts pages of his Sunday paper.

She'd done well, too. The play she had chosen was exactly what he'd have picked for himself—if he'd wanted to go anywhere.

Unfortunately it was the kind of play that Mandy enjoyed, too. They'd talked about the playwright on that first drive out of London, establishing a mutual admiration for a man who was at the top of both their 'must see' lists.

Worse than that, though, far worse than remembering their first meeting, that spark of instant attraction, had been the moment when they had pulled up outside the theatre. The taxi had stopped and he'd paid the driver, organising a pick-up for later, and he'd remembered how, the last time he had done that his heart had been pounding like an adolescent in the throes of calf love, with knees like runny jelly. And with the memory had come the surge of adrenalin, the flight or fight high as he'd known...*known*, that she would be there too. That they would come face to face.

His heart had seemed to know it, and as he'd stepped out of the cab into the sharp cold of the January night he'd discovered that his knees were catching up fast.

Then Sadie had tucked her hand in his arm, and because it was supposed to be a treat, because she was trying so hard to please him, he'd made an effort to smile as he took her into the crush bar so that she could look for celebrities. And of course Mandy hadn't been there.

He wasn't sure which was worse. The swamping hollowness of disappointment. Or, even now, as he scanned the crowd looking for her, the knowledge that he was a fool.

'Dad?' He turned, saw Sadie's anxious expression. 'Are you pleased with your present?'

'Pleased? It's wonderful,' he said. 'Just perfect.'

And that was when he saw her, over Sadie's head, sweeping past the entrance to the bar on the arm of a tall, spare man—dark, like her, but with just a touch of grey at the temples, a cane to support the slightest limp. Exactly the kind of man he would have expected her to be with. A man of the world. Exquisitely tailored, distinguished, and without doubt the possessor of a credit rating that would achieve the stamp of approval from her friendly neighbourhood investigator.

Amanda hadn't wanted to go to the theatre. 'I'm too tired, Max.'

'Rubbish. The baby is beginning to show and you're afraid everyone will stare and wonder what man got that lucky.'

If her brother thought she was falling for that one, marriage must have softened his brain. 'Then they'll have to wonder, darling, and so will you. I am not hiding. Far from it. Setting up the new department means that I'm busier than ever. Which is one of the reasons I'm not in the mood for a night out.' She ran her hand over the curve of her stomach. 'And the baby scarcely shows.'

Max just grinned. 'I'm sorry to disillusion you, poppet, but you look as if you've swallowed a pickled onion whole, and while no one has dared broach the subject with me, at least three people have asked Jilly when your happy event is expected.'

All right. So she had been fooling herself. Not that she'd been going out of her way to hide her pregnancy; she had just hoped not to be the subject of gossip for at least one more month. 'You expect me to go to the theatre with you after that?' she demanded.

'Please, Mandy. Jilly's baby is due in a couple of

weeks, and she can't sit comfortably for more than ten minutes.'

'Then you should stay at home and rub her back.'

'She's not alone. Harriet's with her.'

'A housekeeper is not the same as a husband.'

'How would you know?' Then he dragged his fingers through his hair and she saw that he was on edge. 'God, I'm sorry, Mandy, but do you think I want to leave her right now? It's an Arts Board thing; I have to go.' He smiled coaxingly. 'You can wear that cloak Mother gave you for Christmas. You could hide triplets under that.'

'I'm not hiding!' she declared.

'Prove it. You've got ten minutes to change,' he replied, at which point she surrendered. Just to show him. But as she quickly discarded her first choice of dress she was forced to acknowledge that he was right about her waistline. It was very obvious that she wouldn't be wearing clinging jersey for some time. Oh, well. There were always her earrings. Her hand trailed across the box and, as always, stopped by the compartment with the single jade drop. She should throw it away. One day she would. Maybe.

She was wearing a cloak. Soft, pale grey velvet, gleaming richly in the lights from the chandeliers, covering her from shoulder to ankle. But her neck was white and satin smooth above the collar. He knew all about that neck. He'd touched that neck. Kissed that neck…

Her dark hair skimmed her cheekbones, cut with exquisite precision, every strand in place. Not mussed tonight. No flour tonight.

He'd cupped her head in his hands, held it; his

fingers had tangled the thick silk of her hair as he'd held her close, her hips a cradle for his body. It had smelt of wild flowers and grass… He'd picked dried leaves from her hair. No leaves tonight. And then the light caught the flash of gold at her ear, the long, beaten gold twist of a leaf that brushed against her neck.

Instinctively his hand went to his pocket, to the small piece of jade that he had flung angrily into a bin. And then retrieved. And never quite been able to part with. Definitely a fool.

'Dad?'

Sadie began to turn to see what he was looking at, but he didn't want her to see Mandy, couldn't bear the I-told-you-so look that she wouldn't be able to keep from her eyes. 'Sorry,' he said, the smile an automatic reaction that bore no relevance to the way he was feeling, simply a mask to disguise his pain. And he took the programme. 'I remember,' he said, distracting her, looking at the picture of the actress. 'Wasn't she the one who murdered her husband in that programme about…?' He said the first thing that came into his head and Sadie, with a major sigh, put him right.

When he looked again, Mandy and her companion were being ushered away with unctuous deference by the front of house manager. *Serious* money.

'You're sure you don't want a soft drink?' Max said, indicating the bottles on the small table at the rear of the box.

Amanda shook her head, not really hearing him. Ever since she had arrived at the theatre she had been feeling something. A tingle at the base of her spine.

It had been like that moment, months earlier, when she had been talking to the students at the secretarial college and she had known Daniel had been thinking about her.

He was here. In the theatre. She knew it.

'Mandy?'

'Sorry, Max. Nothing.'

He took her cloak, laid it over one of the chairs, poured himself a drink while Amanda, from her vantage point half hidden behind the dark red velvet drape of the curtain, looked out over the auditorium as it filled with theatregoers. She couldn't see him.

She wouldn't be able to see him. He'd seen her standing in the box as he and Sadie had paused at the entrance to the auditorium to get their bearings. And then he had realised that they would be seated back a little, and out of her line of sight. He wasn't sure whether he was pleased or sorry.

Common sense warned him that he should be feeling nothing, but that wasn't an option open to him. For the first time in his life he had fallen in love. In that last moment before a bright and beautiful future had crumbled to dust in his hands he had told her so, and the words, once launched into the air, could never be recalled or rescinded. They were there for ever, a tiny vibration of sound that would echo through time.

He wasn't there. Her imagination was working overtime, that was all, and imagination had combined with longing, and the knowledge that the theatre was a pleasure they shared, to suggest a scenario where they might, by chance, meet one day. Still dreaming of happy endings. Still dreaming that Daniel might hold his baby and remember that he had said he loved her.

Amanda sighed with relief as the first-night speeches came to a close and the curtain descended for the last time so that she could escape. She just hoped that Max wouldn't expect intelligent conversation about the play she had just sat through, because she had scarcely taken in a word.

'Mandy, I have to put in an appearance backstage. Just for a few minutes. You don't mind, do you?'

'Five minutes. After that I'm taking your car and you're going to have to wait for the driver to come back for you.'

'Five minutes it is. I want to get back to Jilly.' He picked up her cloak and placed it about her shoulders, then he ushered her out into the corridor.

People were still milling about the foyer, gossiping, eager to chat. 'This way,' Max said, taking her by the elbow and leading the way, the little knots of people giving way before him. They were almost through when he stopped, and Amanda, coming alongside him, stopped too.

It was Daniel. Daniel and Sadie. Both of them seemed fixed to the spot, unable to move, and there was a pause that seemed to go on for ever. A wordless exchange. He said nothing, and if he chose not to speak, then neither could she. No matter that she yearned to go to him, push away the concealing velvet and take his hand, place it on her belly and say, *This is your child. Yours and mine. I've already felt him moving inside me like a tiny butterfly…*

Then Max said, 'Look, do you mind? We need to get through there.' It broke the spell that had seemed, for a moment, to hold them in stasis, and Sadie stepped to one side.

Max pushed the door for her and waited for her to go through first, then he followed her, leaving the door to swing shut behind him. 'Heavens,' he said, 'that was a bit tense. The way that man was looking at you…' And then he stopped. Just stopped, half turned but didn't quite meet her eyes. Then he said, 'Do you know, I think we might give this do a miss after all? Once we get backstage we're never going to get away.'

Amanda's lips moved, but for a moment nothing escaped them. Then she cleared her throat and tried again. 'It doesn't matter, Max.' There. It wasn't so difficult. 'You don't have to rush off because of me. I'm fine. Really.' Life went on. 'I've been working far too hard recently. I think a party might be just what I need.' You had to make it go on.

'Dad?' Sadie was still holding his hand. Her fingers had dug in so hard when they had come face to face with Mandy that he could still as they waited for their taxi, feel the imprint of them on his palm. It had only been that pressure stopping him from taking the betraying step towards her, from asking her how she was, simply to hear the sound of her voice. 'Dad, we don't have to go to a restaurant to eat. I could make you an omelette or something.'

She sounded scared. Frightened by the intensity of what had happened back there. Well, it had frightened him. But it wasn't Sadie's fault. None of it was her fault.

And he had to eat. He forced himself do it every day, although he couldn't have said afterwards what he had eaten or what it had tasted like. He only knew that there were a lot of good people depending on him to provide the work that paid their mortgages, put food on their tables. And Sadie needed him, too, so falling apart was not an option. As the car drew up beside them he opened the door and gave the driver the name of the restaurant where he had booked a table. Not Italian. Chinese.

CHAPTER TEN

'AMANDA, you do look well.' Pamela Warburton took her hand, held it warmly for a moment, before taking her into lunch with the staff and the school governors. 'When is the baby due?'

'Mid-June or thereabouts.'

'Your mother must be delighted. Two grandchildren in the space of a year.'

Not as delighted as she'd hoped, Amanda thought, but she was putting a brave face on it.

'I hope you're going to oblige me with a girl. Your sister-in-law isn't in any hurry to put her daughter's name down for Dower House.'

'I don't think Jilly can see the point in having children and then sending them away to boarding school.' Her hand strayed protectively towards the unmistakable curve where her baby lay beneath her breast. Her parents had had little choice with her and Max; her father had been with the Foreign Office and spent long periods of duty abroad. She hadn't been unhappy, but she was on Jilly's side in this one. Fortunately it wasn't going to be a problem. 'And I have to tell you that this little soul wouldn't be entirely welcome. He's a boy,' she said.

'Good grief, Amanda, I thought you were the most organised girl I ever taught. How on earth did you allow that to happen?'

For a moment Amanda thought she was being serious, and then she saw the glint of mischief in the older woman's eyes. 'Just careless, I guess.'

'Can't this old monster go any faster, Dad? We're going to be late.'

'And whose fault is that? You were the one knee deep in your entire wardrobe and enough warpaint to excite Geronimo.'

'Who's Geronimo?'

He wasn't sure whether she was kidding him. 'Never mind. I don't know why you insisted on going to prize-giving anyway. It isn't compulsory and the invitation was nothing but a formality. I can't imagine that Mrs Warburton is expecting you.' He grinned. 'You couldn't possibly have won any prizes.' Now who was doing the teasing?

'It's automatic. Get five As and the book token is yours.'

'Does six get you the cuddly toy?'

'Six just gets you a bigger book token.'

'I can see how that would be a real inducement to sit through a load of speeches and an endless of parade of girls having their hand shaken by some high-achieving old girl.'

He was teasing her. He knew exactly why she'd decided to attend her school prize-giving. It had nothing to do with book tokens and everything to do with the opportunity to appear before her peers wearing a skirt that stopped perilously close to decency, boots laced to the knee and a make-up job that would stop traffic.

He was only glad that Gresham had removed himself from any possibility of temptation, because she looked absolutely stunning, and, rising six feet, there wouldn't be a soul at Dower House who was going to be allowed to miss that fact.

Maybe he should have tried to talk her into something a little less provocative, but she'd tried so hard once she'd gone back to school, had come through her re-sits with honours and was working with such enthusiasm at the garage that he was inclined to indulge her. Allow her to flaunt her success. Pamela Warburton might raise her eyebrows a little, but he didn't for a moment believe that she would deny Sadie her moment of triumph.

'Who is giving the prizes this year?' he asked as he backed the Jaguar into a parking space.

'Some old girl made good.' Sadie fished in her bag for the invitation. 'Amanda Garland,' she said. Dan's foot slipped and the car lurched backwards. He recovered. Shut down the engine. His hand was steady on the key, so it must be everything else that was shaking. Then Sadie shrugged, unfastened her seat belt. 'I've never heard of her.'

'She runs a secretarial agency,' Dan said. 'A very exclusive one. She's used us occasionally to get her temps to important clients.' Not lately, though. And he hadn't followed up to find out if there was some problem.

'What's she like?'

He dragged his attention back to Sadie. 'I've no idea. Let's just hope she's not long-winded.'

There were a number of younger pupils stationed at the entrance to show latecomers into the back of hall. Mrs Warburton was already into the thank-you-for-coming, the-girls-have-done-really-well, we-need-funds-for-the-new-computer-suite speech, and he quickly took a seat in the back row. Sadie had been whisked away by an open-mouthed, wide-eyed junior, presumbly to join the other girls sitting near the front.

Alone in the back row, Dan surveyed the figures on the stage and settled in for the long haul of sports successes, examination results, expansion plans; none of them were of any interest to him. Instead he amused himself trying to decide which of the women seated on the platform was Amanda Garland.

It wasn't very bright of him, because before he could stop it his mind was taking a detour, wandering back to a warm autumn morning when he had teased Mandy Fleming about the old tartar she worked for. It was her voice that haunted him, her quick laughter, the soft cry of pleasure as he'd possessed her. He dragged a hand over his face, as if to wipe away the image, but it wouldn't go. Even as the audience applauded the appearance of the speaker she was there in front of him. Standing at the lectern. Mandy.

'As most of you can see,' she began, 'I really shouldn't be here.' There was the polite laughter of an audience not quite sure where they were being taken. 'My mission, I have been told, is to inspire the Dower House girls with the "you-can-have-it-all" ethos of today. Well, girls, I'm here to tell you that I do have it all. Backache, swollen ankles, heartburn…' The laughter increased. Self-ridicule was a well-established British institution.

Mandy. He didn't understand. It was Mandy.

'It wouldn't matter, of course, if I could stay at home and put my feet up. But having it all means that no matter how bad the backache, how swollen the ankles, how sleepless the night, I have to be out of bed by seven and in my office by eight-thirty.' She smiled around at her audience. 'Of course I wouldn't have it any other way. Running the Garland Agency is my life…' She made that instinctively protective gesture that all women use when they are pregnant. *Pregnant?* He began to rise. 'But my life is just about to get very complicated. So. Is the dream possible? I'm going to ask you today to think about what it means for a woman who wants to have everything…'

Amanda paused as someone at the rear of the hall stood up. Paused and looked. And then she wished she hadn't. She'd put the tantalising tingle down to the extra weight she was carrying. Ignored it. Stupid. Because now she was standing before a packed auditorium, six months pregnant, and the father of her child was standing at the back of the room looking at her as if he had seen an apparition. And if Daniel was here, then it followed that Sadie must be, too.

'Are you all right, Amanda?' She heard Pamela Warburton's anxious whisper at her shoulder. She'd put her feet up in Pamela's sitting room after lunch and dozed off, and the head had suggested she stay there during the introductions, the school speeches. She hadn't needed much persuasion. She looked well enough, but she found she was needing more rest as the weeks passed and sitting for half an hour on an upright wooden chair wasn't going to do anything for her swollen ankles.

Was she all right? No, she certainly wasn't all right, but she took a sip of water and then carried on, resolutely avoiding making eye contact with the far corner of the room. Short of fainting, there wasn't anything else she could do. And since she had never fainted in her life, the likelihood of rescue coming from that direction seemed remote.

Dan, once the surge of adrenalin that had brought

him to his feet had subsided, sank back onto the chair. Mandy Fleming. Amanda Garland. How could he have been so stupid?

And why hadn't she told him? Why, when he'd given her all that rubbish, hadn't she just told him who she was and put him in his place?

Because he'd flirted with her and she'd been amused. He remembered the things he'd said and knew he should be grateful she'd been amused. And because she'd been amused she'd flirted right back, and before either of them had realised it had all got out of hand.

He hadn't had to go back to pick her up that first evening. He could have arranged something. He just hadn't been able to help himself. But he'd wanted her to love him for himself. And while he had been guiltily protecting himself from a designing temp with her sights set on a man with money, Miss Amanda Garland had been protecting her own assets from a chauffeur on the make.

Amanda Garland. Her truth. That was what she had been about to tell him when Sadie had appeared at the cottage like the wicked witch in a pantomime.

And she was pregnant. She was having his baby and because of what he'd said she'd kept it from him. Even when he'd seen her at the theatre…

Damn! Why hadn't he noticed then? And who the hell had been her expensive-looking date? Jealousy welled up like thick poison…

Had Sadie noticed? Was that why her fingers had dug like claws into his hand, stopping him from making a move… Sadie. Once more the adrenalin hit him like a sledgehammer and this time he was out of his chair like a rocket. It took him no time at all to see that Sadie was not in the room. Who could miss her?

'Excuse me, sir? Can I help you?'

One of the junior moppets, washed and brushed and shining for the occasion, cut him off as he stepped out into the corridor and headed for backstage. It was the child who had whisked Sadie away. 'I need to speak to my daughter,' he said. 'It's urgent.' She looked blank. 'The tall girl in black. With the spiky hair.'

The child sucked in a long breath. 'Sadie Redford? She is way cool.'

Maybe, but the eruption of applause signalling the end of Mandy's speech meant that he was running out of time. Sadie was about to walk onto the stage and be confronted by Mandy. Amanda. And no amount of cool could possibly prepare her for that. 'My daughter?' he prompted.

'She went to the cloakroom,' the child said.

'Where is it?'

'You can't go in there!'

Amanda was feeling hot. Hot and a bit swimmy. She would have liked to sit down but suspected that would appear wimpish. There was just the handing out of certificates and prizes to be got through and Pamela Warburton had that down to a fine art, not permitting clapping to interrupt the speedy dishing out of honours. Proud parents had to wait until the end before they could show their delight.

Name, certificate, handshake. Name, certificate, handshake. Name, certificate, handshake. After a while it had a certain hypnotic quality.

He banged on the door. 'Sadie!' No answer. He pushed it open but there were no screams of outrage. The place was empty. He'd missed her. Oh, God. He didn't need this. He needed to be thinking about the fact that he was about to become a father. He needed to be thinking about it, deciding what to do, working out how he felt, how he was ever going to convince the woman he loved that he wasn't the bastard he seemed.

Instead he raced back to the hall just in time to hear the assistant head call out her name. 'Mercedes Redford'. Like a man watching an accident about to happen and totally unable to do anything to stop it, he watched as she climbed the three steps up the platform, walked across to the table. And he winced as he saw the moment that she realised who was on the other end of the handshake.

Amanda had known it was coming. As the names had crept up through the alphabet. What she didn't know was whether Sadie had seen her, whether she was prepared. The girls were supposed to sit in the hall and listen to the speaker, but she'd been there, done that, and knew that the older girls always had better things to do than listen to some boring adult exhorting them to great things. And it was clear the moment Sadie saw her that it was a total shock, that she hadn't known.

Not even Sadie would have deliberately let drop the word that escaped her in such company. 'You're not Amanda Garland, you're Mandy Fleming. The earring queen.' The expletive she inserted in such ringing tones between the word 'the' and the word 'earring' brought a sharp intake of breath from the entire assembly. And, having got everyone's undivided attention, she added, 'Oh my God, you're pregnant.'

Amanda might have made it a rule in life never to faint, but there were exceptions to every rule. This was plainly one of them, and she had better do it quickly before Sadie decided to enlighten her enrapt audience with the name of the father of her child. Actually, it was a lot easier than she had anticipated to allow herself to slide, with such grace as her condition permitted, to the floor. The fact that Daniel Redford was moving purposefully towards them, his face set in an expression that boded nothing but trouble, certainly helped.

If he had been harbouring any doubts about his feelings for Mandy, or for the baby she was carrying, the sight of her slumping to the floor sorted them out for him in short order. He covered the endless stretch of polished floor that led to the platform in a rush, took the steps in one stride, and the women on the platform who had instinctively surged forward to help fell back to let him through.

'Call an ambulance,' he barked out as he bent over her, loosened the soft silk scarf about her throat and felt for her pulse. 'Mandy…' He murmured her name. 'Come on, my darling girl…' He reached for the tumbler of water, soaked the corner of her scarf and laid it over her forehead, moistened her lips. 'Sweetheart, please…' Her eyes flickered, briefly met his, and at that moment he realised that she was faking it, drawing attention from Sadie.

Relief surged through him, along with a surge of emotions so mixed that he didn't know what to say first. *Forgive me.* Or, *Thank you.* Or, *Don't you ever scare me like that again as long as you live.* 'I love you,' he murmured. 'I missed you so much.'

Amanda thought that she might cry. But breaking one rule a day was quite enough. 'Don't be silly,' she muttered. 'I'll be fine. Just look after Sadie.' He continued to grip her hand. 'She needs you, Daniel.'

'And you don't?'

Oh, the temptation! But she'd given her word... 'Sadie,' she persisted, although she knew her heart would break this time for sure.

'Sadie?' He finally glanced round, but his daughter had taken advantage of the confusion to make her escape.

'Go and find her, Daniel,' Mandy urged.

Pamela Warburton nodded. 'I'll look after her,' she said. 'Go and find Sadie before she does something stupid.'

'It's a bit late for that.' Daniel continued to look down at her for another few moments, then he squeezed her hand. 'I'll be back,' he said. 'And I'll be wanting some answers.'

Daniel was silently directed by the moppet in the direction of the cloakroom. Yes, well, his darling daughter would undoubtedly prefer to face the wrath of Pamela Warburton right now, but if she thought that hiding out in the girls' cloakroom would save her she was mistaken, and he pushed open the door.

Sadie had her back pressed against the cold white tiles, tears flowing down her ashen face, and she made no sign to indicate that she knew he was there, keeping her eyes straight ahead. 'She did it, then,' she said. 'I tried to stop it, but now you'll have to marry her, too.'

'Stop it? What do you mean, stop it?'

'Honestly, Dad, haven't you heard of safe sex?' she demanded.

'Was it safe sex that you were offering Ned Gresham when you stripped off in the Lexus?'

Her mouth fell open. 'I just wanted to... He wouldn't...'

'I know exactly what you wanted to do. You wanted to punish your mother by getting pregnant.'

'There's a lot of it about,' Sadie replied, then coloured crimson. Dan thought that was promising. He'd have sworn she didn't know how. 'Was that why he left? Did you fire him?' she demanded. 'It wasn't his fault... I just wanted...'

'I know what you wanted. And, no, I didn't fire him. He didn't rat on you, either. When I realised you'd gone out, I came looking for you. I thought he handled an awkward situation very well.'

She groaned and slumped against the wall. 'And I thought the day couldn't get any worse.'

'Oh, I don't think we're there by a long shot yet, sweetheart.' He put his arm around her, pulled her against him, held her for a moment. 'What did you do?'

'Do?'

'You said you tried to stop it. Mandy and me. What did you do?'

She mumbled something against his chest. He wasn't sure he'd heard right and leaned back. 'Swear? What did you make her swear?'

She straightened, looked him in the eyes. 'I promised I'd go back to school if she swore never to see you again.'

She hadn't told him because she'd promised Sadie? Could it be that simple? 'After the way I treated her that day?' he said. And his blood ran cold at the memory. 'Did you really think she would ever want to see me again?'

Sadie's eyes flashed up him. 'Why wouldn't she? You're everything she wants…'

'You're missing what happened here today, Sadie. She doesn't need me. Not for money, anyway. She's Amanda Garland. A successful business woman in her own right.' But maybe, if he was lucky, she would realise she needed him in other ways.

'Then why—'

'Why was she checking up on me? I allowed her to think I was a simple chauffeur. I wanted to be loved for myself, not my bank balance. She was simply protecting herself from the chance that I might have been looking for a rich wife.'

'But—'

But he'd explained enough. 'Why do you persist in calling her the earring queen?'

'Because she thinks she looks so—' There was an abrupt pause as Sadie bit back the expletive. 'Because she thinks she looks so wonderful wearing the stupid things.' Then she shrugged. 'Because she does look wonderful. She's beautiful, and you look at her like she's a queen.'

'And?'

Sadie shifted uncomfortably, then finally met his gaze. 'Because you still carry one of them with you everywhere you go. You're never without it. I'm jealous. And I'm scared that you'll leave me like Mum did.' She finally broke down and sobbed against his chest. 'I'm so sorry, Dad. I'm so sorry. You're in love with her and I've ruined it for you.'

'I think perhaps that was something of a joint effort. That amount of trouble takes three. But maybe it's not beyond salvage.' He found a handkerchief, soaked it and wiped the mascara from her face. 'I am, however, going to need your assistance.'

'Haven't I done enough?'

'Not quite.' He turned with her towards the door. 'Come on. Time to face the music.' Her response was brief and to the point. 'You know, sweetheart, I'd have thought someone who managed a starred A for English was well beyond the need to rely on bad language to make a point.' She didn't answer him. 'It's just as well you never made the Roll of Honour, or they'd have had to paint out your name.' He grinned. 'Still, after today's performance I don't suppose it will ever be forgotten. You'll have achieved legendary status by next term. New girls will be told what happened in hushed tones after lights-out…' But the last of his words were drowned out by the arrival, sirens wailing, of the ambulance.

Sadie, her face finally lifting into a sheepish smile, spun round to face him, her expression frozen in horror. 'The baby!' Then, with a wail of such remorse that it tore into his heart, she cried out, 'What have I done? You should be with her…' And before he could stop her she broke yet another sacred school rule as she turned and ran along the corridor.

Amanda was sitting quietly in Pamela Warburton's sitting room having her blood pressure checked by the paramedic. She had protested that there was no need. That it had all been a mistake. She just wanted to find Daniel, to reassure Sadie, but the paramedic wasn't letting her go without giving her the once-over. 'Better safe than sorry,' he said, and had just fitted the cuff to her arm when Sadie burst in.

'The baby? Is the baby going to be all right?'

'Mercedes!'

But she was impervious to Pamela Warburton's admonition. 'Mandy… Miss Fleming… Miss Garland… I'm so sorry. I've been so stupid. Please, please don't blame Dad for what happened. It was all my fault. I was just so scared you were going to take him away from me—'

Amanda saw that Daniel had followed her into the room, and now Sadie turned to him.

'Tell her how much you love her. Tell her about the earring,' she implored.

'Do tell her, old man. And while you're about it, maybe someone would tell me what the devil is going on.'

'Max!' Amanda greeted the arrival of her brother with relief. Escape was but a heartbeat away.

Or maybe not, she realised as Daniel turned to confront him. 'And who the devil are you?' he demanded.

'Maxim Fleming.' Max extended his hand. 'Didn't we almost meet at the theatre a couple of months back?'

'Fleming?' Daniel looked from Mandy to the new arrival.

'I'm Mandy's brother.' And Max smiled. 'In case you were wondering.'

Belatedly Daniel took the proferred hand. 'Daniel Redford,' he said. 'I'm going to marry your sister.'

'Really?'

Mandy groaned as Max turned to her.

'And you didn't say a word when I dropped you off before lunch.'

'He hadn't asked me before lunch.' Amanda had her face buried in her hands. 'In fact, unless I missed something, I'm pretty sure he hasn't asked me at all.'

'I'm asking you now. Will you marry me?'

The room was full of people. All of them waiting for her answer. How could he do that to her? How could the sensible, organised, totally in control Amanda Garland have ever got herself into this situation? She pulled herself together, looked him straight in the eyes… beautiful, hazy blue-grey eyes… 'Don't be silly, Daniel. The last thing I need is a husband.'

'Strike one.' Max raised his brows and glanced pointedly around at Pamela Warburton, the school matron, two paramedics and Sadie. 'Who said romance was dead?' he murmured.

'You proposed to Jilly in front of the buffet car queue on an Intercity train,' Amanda retorted, leaping to Daniel's defence. 'How romantic was that?'

Max grinned. 'Romantic enough,' he said. 'She said yes.' Then he turned to Daniel. 'My apologies. Do carry on.'

Daniel turned to her. 'This has got nothing to do with the fact that you're having my baby. I've had the worst six months of my life without you.'

'There is the possibility that it would have been worse with me,' she said.

'Strike two.'

'Go away, Max. All of you, go away. This is doing my blood pressure no good at all.'

'Your blood pressure is fine, miss.' The paramedic

released the cuff and began to stow it away. Very slowly.

'Please listen to him.' Sadie's voice was small, but Daniel heard it and Mandy heard it and, despite her protestations, he knew it would be all right. The woman he loved was with him, holding his gaze with a look that said it all. It said, *Whew.* And, *We nearly messed that up.* And, *I love you so much that living without you was like losing a limb.* Behind her eyes she was smiling, even though her face was serious. 'It's your life,' Sadie said, more forcefully. 'And Dad's. I'll be going away to university in a couple of years and then he's going to need someone to…um…well, you know…' Mandy's hand flew to her cover her mouth, as if to hide a smile. Yes, well, they did know. 'And then there's the baby. It is really going to be all right?' she asked anxiously.

'He's going to be fine.'

'He?'

Amanda nodded. 'I've seen the scan. Here, give me your hand.' And she took Sadie's hand and placed it on her stomach and let her feel the baby kick.

'But that's…that's amazing.' She turned to her father. 'Come and feel the baby move.' Still Dan waited. He'd seen all the answer he wanted in Mandy's eyes and he understood exactly what she was doing. Why she was waiting. 'For heaven's sake, Dad,' Sadie said impatiently. 'What are you waiting for?'

Then Sadie, too, caught up with what was going on, and with a huge sigh, she said, 'Oh, right.' And she stood up and crossed to her father, took his arm for a moment and kissed his cheek. 'Of course Mandy's going to marry you.' Then she grinned. 'If she says no, just tell her she can't have her earring back; that should fix her.' And she crossed to the door and opened it. 'But I'm sure she'd rather give you her answer…' she looked pointedly around at the interested spectators '…without an audience.'

For a long moment after the door closed there was only silence. Daniel was the first to break it. 'Would you have told me? About the baby?'

Would she? 'I wanted to tell you, Daniel. I knew I should, that you'd want to know, but I promised Sadie—'

'Promised Sadie?' He looked stunned. 'But she didn't know—'

'No!' She put out a hand to stop him. 'No,' she repeated, more gently. 'It was at the cottage. She was scared, Daniel, and fierce as any tiger guarding her cub. There was no way she was going back to school and leaving you prey to some scheming woman. So I promised her that if she went back to school I would stay away from you. It was the least I could do. And I didn't think it would matter. I didn't think you would give me the time of day—'

'You still haven't answered my question. Would you have told me about the baby?'

She hadn't answered because she didn't know what she might have done once her child was born. She suspected that she wouldn't have had to do anything. She gave a little shrug. 'I promised Sadie, but Beth didn't. I imagine she was planning to drop you a congratulations card… Not very subtle, but then she's an incurable romantic.'

'This is the friend with the flat in Shepherd's Bush?'

'Friend. Business partner. It was Beth who had you checked out.'

'Not that much of a romantic, then.'

'She was protecting me from myself.' She'd always known she was going to have to tell him the truth. So she did. It didn't take long.

'You wanted my baby but not me?'

'For about thirty seconds. Then I wanted you on any terms. I hadn't read the report, Daniel. Actually, I never did get to read it,' she said, when he didn't speak. 'Maybe I should ask you what your prospects are before I consider your proposal,' she prompted. 'That's if you're still proposing?'

A promising smile tugged at the corner of his mouth. 'You are considering it, then?'

'Do you really carry my earring around with you?' she asked.

He reached inside his jacket pocket and produced a small fold of tissue paper. Inside it was her jade earring. She held out her hand for it, but he shook his head. 'It goes with a ring.' He crossed the room, came to his knees beside her. 'You wanted my baby, Mandy. Well, I'm here to tell you that we come as a package, sweetheart.' And he laid his hand gently on the mound where his baby was growing. His eyes widened as the baby moved. 'Hey! He kicked! You're growing a footballer.'

'Not a dancer?' He looked up sharply and she laughed. 'He's not kicking, he's just saying hello.' Then she stopped teasing and her eyes filled, her throat tightened as she said, 'He's saying, ''Hello, Daddy''.'

He took her hand between his. 'Then I'd say my

prospects are just fine. And maybe next time it'll be a girl. She can be a dancer, if you like.'

'Chauvinist.'

He grinned. 'You bet.'

'You don't have to marry me, you know. Not just because of the baby.'

'Sweetheart, this is nothing to do with the baby. When I saw you standing by the Silver Ghost, I knew right then that I wanted you sitting in the back going to church for me. And it didn't take me six months to discover that life without you was going to be hell. Maybe if I hadn't been so eaten with jealousy that you were with another man, I would have noticed your waistline at the theatre.'

'I was wearing a cloak. Everything was well hidden.' Still self-conscious. 'Would it have made a difference?'

'It would have given me the excuse I needed to ignore all the sensible stuff my brain was telling me and listen to my heart.' He was holding onto her hand so tightly she was beginning to lose feeling in her fingers. 'Look, are you going to marry me, or what? There are half a dozen people out there waiting for your answer.'

'They can wait a few more minutes.' Amanda's smile was slow and full of love. 'Right now, Daniel Redford, the only thing I want is for you to stop talking and kiss me.'

'Well done, Tom!'

'See, football's not so bad,' Daniel said. 'Is it?' Amanda glanced up at Daniel and saw that he was grinning from ear to ear as she restrained herself from giving the boy a hug in front of his team mates.

'This isn't football. This is family stuff.' She looped her arm through his as they walked back to the car. 'And next week you get your turn to applaud Molly, when her ballet class puts on a show.'

He bent and scooped up his four-year-old daughter in his free arm and blew a soft raspberry into her neck, making her giggle. 'I can't wait. I love family stuff.'

'Talking of family stuff, have you spoken to Sadie? Did she say if she was coming home for Christmas?'

'Yes. And she's bringing someone with her. She wouldn't say who, but I have the feeling it's a boyfriend. A serious boyfriend.'

'Can you handle that?'

'Can I handle the prospect of becoming a grandfather? No problem.'

'Then as a reward I've got a special present for you.'

Daniel stopped, put Molly down so that she could run and join her brother. 'An early Christmas present?'

'No, you'll have to wait for your birthday for this one.'

'My birthday isn't for seven months.'

'Well, anticipation is half the fun. Did I ever explain to you about the demographics of population?'

'Falling birth rate, that kind of thing?'

'That's right. I thought you'd be glad to know that we're doing our best to compensate.'

'Is that right?' He glanced at her waistline, then, grinning, met her gaze. 'And we'll be compensating on my birthday, will we?'

'Can you handle that?'

'Oh, yes, sweetheart. I'm really getting the hang of the fatherhood bit. Can you?'

'Just as long as you're there to hold my hand.'

'Always.' And as Daniel's arm tightened about her waist and he drew her close, breathing a kiss against her cheek, Amanda remembered the first time they'd met, how she'd imagined four little babies wrapped in white with blue ribbons, each one with smoky-blue eyes and a lop-sided smile.

Three down, she thought, with a secret little smile. One to go.